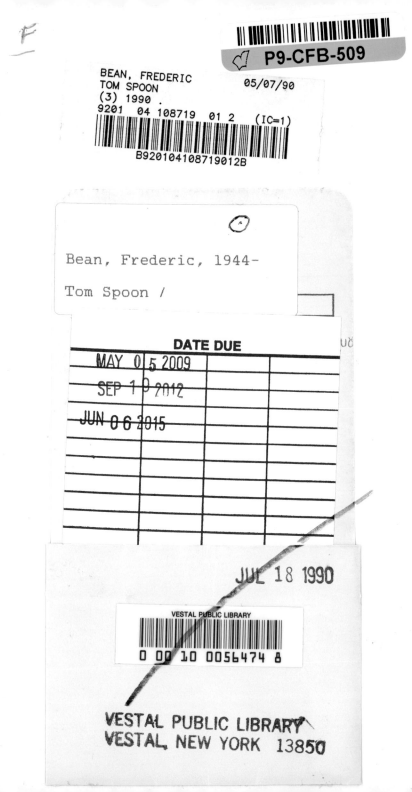

TOM SPOON

Frederic Bean

Walker and Company
New York

First published in the United States of America in 1990
by Walker Publishing Company, Inc.

Published simultaneously in Canada by Thomas Allen & Son
Canada, Limited, Markham, Ontario

Library of Congress Cataloging-in-Publication Data

Bean, Frederic, 1944–
Tom Spoon / Frederic Bean.
ISBN 0-8027-4103-7
I. Title.
PS3552.B152T6   1990   813′.54—dc20   89-70478

CHAPTER 1

THE stallion walled his eyes when he felt the weight of the cowboy. Slim held the snubbing rope for the cowboy; the rope was dallied, too tight for the horse to make his first move until Slim flipped the rope off the saddlehorn. When the rope was in the rider's hands, Slim reined his gelding out of harm's way and got set to watch the action. Not a single bronc stomper within fifty miles had ever survived more than two jumps on the grey stud, not in the ten years that Slim could vouch for. Watching cowboys make a try at riding Big Blue was the best Sunday entertainment in the Concho valley.

The grey squealed, like he always did when he was about to send a rider among the sparrows, then he dropped his massive head and kicked higher than the rider's hat. Slim recalled he had never seen a horse with so much power, enough to unseat the best horsemen in middle Texas. The old man astraddle Big Blue didn't have a snowball's chance in hell of making the second jump. Slim knew it. The other hands gathered around the corral fence knew it.

Big Blue bawled and jumped, sunfishing, twisting his back and hindquarters. Slim admired the rider's style as the old cowboy raked his spurs across the grey's shoulders. Slim would have bet the silver- haired gent rode his share of rank broncs to a standstill in his day. He had balance, and he timed his moves like a man who understood pitching horses.

The grey landed hard, gathering his front legs for another lunge. Slim blinked, surprised to find the old man still in the

1

saddle. Squealing, the stud made a jump halfway across the corral, kicking high enough to give most men a nosebleed.

Spurs raked down the stud's shoulders again. The old man hardly seemed shaken when the grey landed. Rowels clanked against the horse's hide when the spurs went to the point of the shoulder.

Damn, Slim thought when the stallion reared for another try.

A third jump went higher still, then Big Blue whirled into a spin, bawling like a fresh-branded calf, downing his head. The rider sat his saddle, spurring, drawing a trickle of blood from the stud's dappled coat.

"Damn," Slim mumbled to himself.

Just then the stallion sucked back, changing the direction of his spin. It should have almost been enough to jerk the arm of the rider from its socket when it happened so quickly. This was considered a dirty move for a bronc horse to make, something a bronc rider would expect from the worst spoiled outlaw.

Slim blinked again. The rider hadn't even lost his hat with the move. The old man was making it look easy, rocking back and forth in perfect time with the horse.

From one side of the pen to the other, Big Blue did his best: bawling, wringing his tail, landing with enough force to split the rider in half. Slim glanced at the rider's face. A grin was spread over the leathery skin, wrinkling into a web of lines.

"He's laughing," Slim said, bewildered by it. "He's enjoying himself."

Someone hooted along the fence.

"Ride him, cowboy," another cheered.

Slim couldn't believe his eyes. A frail-looking old man was riding Big Blue longer than any man in the Concho valley, a gent old enough to be somebody's grandpa.

The cheering grew louder around the fence. Hats were tossed in the air and under the grey's hooves. The men were seeing a sight no one had ever witnessed before. Someone was riding the most famous bucking horse west of the Leon River, a feat said to be impossible among bronc stompers in the region.

Slim tried to remember the old man's name and couldn't. When the cowboy had ridden up to the ranch on a rawboned dun gelding, asking for a chance to ride Big Blue, Slim had almost dismissed the idea. The man had to be close to sixty. It didn't seem a fair match, the grey against the old-timer. Seeing as it was Sunday, Slim went along with the idea, willing to risk the fifty dollars the ranch would pay if someone rode the stud. It had been a standing offer for so many years Slim had forgotten just when the boss first announced he would pay a reward of fifty dollars to any man who could sit atop Big Blue until he quit bucking.

The grey made a final desperate lunge and stopped, blowing wind through his nostrils, flanks heaving. The rider sat where he had begun the affair, squarely in the middle of his saddle.

"Whoa there," he said, running a calloused hand through the stallion's mane, a gentle pat, the way you might stroke a tomcat's back.

"Damn," Slim said again, disbelieving what he had just seen.

The rider carefully swung a leg over and stepped to the ground, and then rubbed the grey's muzzle affectionately.

"Hell of a horse," he said. "I 'spect he's dumped his share of good men. Tricky bastard, with a lot of heart."

Slim pulled off his hat to sleeve sweat from his brow.

"Never was rode in ten years," Slim replied, " 'til you done it just then. You've earned your fifty dollars, fair an' square. I'll ride up to the house an' tell the bossman he owes you."

The cowboy gave a nod and reached for the cinch. "I'll undress him while you're about it," he said. "You might make mention to the boss I'm lookin' for work."

"We've already got ourselves a wrangler," Slim said, "but we could use a man who swings a rope."

"I've done my share," the cowboy replied.

"Give me your name again," Slim said, "so I can tell the boss who rode Big Blue."

"Name's Spoon. . . . I go by Tom most the time."

Slim hesitated. The name sounded familiar in a vague way, but he couldn't recall where he'd heard it before. He examined the old man's face, trying to remember.

"Tom Spoon . . . right unusual name," Slim said. "Heard it before some place. Can't put a finger on just where or when."

"Not many of us Spoons around," the cowboy replied in a quiet voice, and when he said it Slim thought he detected a touch of worry.

"Could be it'll come to me," Slim said. "I'll ride to the main house and get your pay." Then he rode out of the corral and spurred to a lope up a gentle grade leading to a sprawling ranch house.

One of the hands came up to Tom Spoon to take the lead rope on Big Blue.

"That was one hell of a ride," the bow-legged, lanky cowboy said to Tom as he ran a hand under the stud's jaw to scratch the soft flesh. "Never figured it could be done. I've tried him three times since I hired on with this outfit. Damn near broke me in two the last time. Fact is, you made it look easy."

The cowboy swung around to face Tom and stuck out his hand.

"I'm Bill Hancock. They tell me I'm the horse wrangler at the Triangle Bar. Sometimes, I ain't so sure."

"Tom Spoon," he said as they shook hands.

"Come over to the shed and meet some of the boys," Bill said. "Slim'll be down with your money shortly, when the bossman gets over the shock."

Tom followed as Bill led the stud through the corral gate to a tree-shaded barn where rows of stalls faced a warm westerly wind. Better than a dozen cowboys stood in groups, slouched around the horse shed, talking about the ride as Tom approached. They tossed quick glances Tom's way.

"Boys," Bill said, "meet Tom Spoon. He's the hombre we'll be talking about for a spell . . . when folks ask who rode Blue."

There followed a scattering of howdys and howdy-dos from the men, and remarks like "nice ride," and so on. Tom acknowledged them all with a tip of his hat brim before he leaned against a live oak trunk, hitching his thumbs in his front pockets to wait for Slim to return.

"Believe I know you from some place, Mr. Spoon," an older cowboy said, after a study of Tom's face. "You ever spend any time around Waco?"

Tom stiffened a little, out of habit.

"Time or two," he answered.

The cowboy deliberated for a time before continuing. "Seems I recall a feller by the name of Spoon killed a man over in Waco . . . it was some time back, maybe '78 or '79. Been nigh onto a dozen years, but I remember it. I was there. Seen the whole thing."

When Tom offered no reply, the cowboy went on.

"Right there on Webster Street . . . right in front of The Brazos Queen Dancehall," he said, like it was a question.

Tom waited silently, certain there would be more.

"I'd near 'bout swear the feller's name was Tom Spoon," he added, boring through Tom with a look. "If my memory serves me right, they sent this Spoon down to state prison for a stretch. Talk was, Spoon got railroaded by a hand-picked jury, made up of the dead man's friends. That was the talk around town, best I remember."

Tom waited, figuring the next question before it arrived.

"Could it be you're that same Tom Spoon?" the cowboy asked.

Instead of answering, Tom swung a look toward the ranch house as he heard the clatter of horseshoes. Slim had started back toward the barn, hurrying more than Tom felt the occasion warranted.

"That'll be my money," Tom said to the cowboys. "I reckon I'll be movin' on. You boys toss that ol' grey stud an extra bait of grain for his supper. He's earned it. That's one mighty fine horse you've got."

Slim galloped up to the shed and swung down, fixing Tom with a look before he handed Tom a handful of bills.

"The boss wants to see you up at the house," he said, a changed expression on his face. "He said he'd be obliged if you'd ride up."

Tom pocketed the money and started for his horse, which was tied in the shade of a live oak.

"I'll stop by on my way out," Tom said, swinging a leg over his old high-backed saddle. "Much obliged for the hospitality."

Tom spurred up the slope, wondering why it was necessary to go up to the house, feeling the eyes of the cowhands on his back when he rode away from the barn. He had not answered the question he was asked and he figured they were wondering about him, about the killing over at Waco. Before he dismounted in front of the porch he decided he had not ridden far enough west to escape his past. It was best to move on. With the fifty dollars in his pocket he could strike out for the New Mexico territory, or maybe even make the ride to California if he took the notion.

When his boot hit the first step, the front door swung wide

and a thick-muscled gent of fifty or so came out to greet him, wearing a curious grin.

"Jack Johnson," the man said, shaking Tom's hand. "I asked Slim to invite you up to the house . . . wanted to shake the feller's hand who rode my grey stud. I've got a bottle of good whiskey on a shelf I've been savin' for a special occasion. Never figured I'd be drinkin' to the man who rode Blue . . . didn't think it could be done. Step inside and we'll pull the cork."

Tom hesitated. After the discovery that his reputation was known this far west he tossed aside the idea of seeking daywork in these parts. Best to move on, now that he had fifty dollars in traveling money.

"I hadn't oughta," Tom said. "I'd planned to cover some ground. Much obliged for the offer, anyway."

The rancher's face clouded.

"Slim said you were lookin' for work, Mr. Spoon. I've got a proposition for you, if you're interested in wages."

It was a powerful temptation. For weeks he had stopped at one cow outfit and then another, without any luck. Fall roundups were still a few months away and nobody had a job for a drifter. Right up 'til this morning he'd been worried about starvation, without a cent to his name after paying for the four-dollar horse. Now he suddenly found himself with fifty dollars and an offer of a job.

"I'll listen," Tom said, questioning his quick good fortune.

They entered a richly furnished front room where the rancher showed Tom to a chair, then brought from a cupboard a pair of cigars and a bottle with two shotglasses stacked over the lip.

"This is Kentucky corn juice," he said, pouring while Tom held a match to his cigar, "but it kicks like a Tennessee mule. Smooth goin' down, but it'll take a feller's brain and wring every drop of sense out of it. Here's to the man who rode Big Blue. Wish the hell I coulda seen it."

Tom tasted his drink and allowed a moment for it to sink to his belly. "Smooth as mother's milk," he said before he downed the rest. "Tell me about this job you made mention of."

Johnson settled back in his chair after he'd poured another round, appraising Tom with a look.

"You could be just the feller for the job, Mr. Spoon. Before I tell you about the pay, let me tell you about a problem I've got on my hands. Just hear me out first, before you make up your mind."

Tom studied the rancher's face. It was the mention of a problem that caught Tom's attention, making him wary.

"I raise good horses, Mr. Spoon," he began. "There's some who'll say I run the best string of broodmares in a hundred miles any direction. Triangle Bar cowhorses bring a top price in these parts, mainly because they're honest horses and I stand behind every one I sell. My word's been good in the Concho valley for a considerable spell. If you'll ask around, I figure folks will say the same, if it matters."

He took a drink and let his gaze fall vacantly out a window.

"Early this spring, I found myself at odds with the Texas and Pacific railroad," he went on. "They want a right-of-way through my ranch for a line to El Paso, but if I sold 'em the stretch they want, I'd be cut off from water for my south pastures. Water's one hell of a problem out here, if you didn't know."

Johnson took a puff from his cigar and blew the smoke toward the ceiling.

"I was never one to stand in the way of progress," he continued, "but the land is mine and I figure I've got a right to say no to a railroad. Which is exactly what I did, back in the spring. That's when my troubles started. Two of my hands were shot right out of their saddles, dead as fence posts. Good men . . . been with me for years . . . good friends to boot. I took the matter to the sheriff. I might as well have gone and butted a stump like a locoed billygoat. He made a show of investigating the affair and said he couldn't come up with a thing . . . maybe Mexican bandits, he said, like he figured to play me for a fool. The Texas and Pacific has bought and paid for themselves a sheriff. And they've hired themselves some mighty fancy shootists to back their play."

He let a silence pass, staring out the window before he went on.

"I sent a wire to the Texas Rangers," he added. "Seems politics can get in the way of the law when the stakes are high enough. They sent a pair of Rangers out here . . . asked some questions for a day or two and then rode off. Said it was just my bad luck and they couldn't find a thing. I know better. That railroad camp is full of gunslicks and hardcases the like of which you never saw before. I rode over for a talk with 'em. Saw it for myself."

Tom emptied his glass. The conversation was taking a turn in the wrong direction. It wasn't daywork Johnson had in mind; he was looking for a hired gun.

"I don't aim to take on the railroad," Johnson said. "All I'm after is to be left alone to raise my horses. I've owned this spread for better'n thirty years. It's mine. I damn sure don't have to sell a right-of-way through it to anybody."

Then the rancher turned to Tom and held him with a look.

"I need a man who can handle himself," he said. "My boys are cowhands. Hardly a one of them knows which end of a gun shoots lead. I need a man who can keep an eye on things, so I don't lose another friend to a drygulcher's bullet."

A long silence followed.

"I wouldn't be the right man," Tom said. "I can swing a loop and ride a bronc in passable fashion."

Johnson's eyes twinkled with humor before Tom finished. "No need to be so modest, Mr. Tom Spoon," he said. "According to the stories, before you went to prison you were one of the best."

Tom rubbed his knees, feeling the ache from the jolting bronc ride. It surprised him that anyone knew his reputation so far from his home range, especially after so many years locked away in a prison cell.

"A man can get too old for some things," he said. "Like women . . . or guns. I'm done with both, I reckon. Time changes a man. Too old and worn out for a woman to take a fancy to me, and too slow to make a living with a gun. If I can find work, likely I'll spend the rest of my days with horses and cattle, if my past will leave me alone."

"It can be hard to shake sometimes, Mr. Spoon. When a gent earns himself a reputation, it follows him like a shadow."

Then the rancher rubbed his chin and looked thoughtful.

"Tell you what," Johnson said. "I could use a hand with the fall branding, seein' as I'm two men short. I pay fifteen a month and found. If you've a hankerin' to stay and swing a loop for the Triangle Bar, hang your gear in the bunkhouse and tell Bill to let you have the pick of three geldings. Won't be no more said about this other matter. I'll find a way to handle it myself, if I'm able."

Tom considered it. This was the first job offer he'd had in the weeks since he'd walked through prison gates. With no place else to go, it didn't seem such a bad idea. The Triangle Bar was a place to hang his hat for a spell.

CHAPTER 2

BILL Hancock eyed Tom closely as Tom hung his warbag from a peg in the bunkhouse.

"Snuffy claims you were a gunfighter," Bill said. "I ain't a nosy sort, but I was wonderin' if there was any truth to what Snuffy says."

Tom set his jaw to help control his anger over everyone's insistence on bringing up what he wanted to forget.

"Could be I'm the same one," he said evenly, biting down on the words.

"You sign on to help us fight them railroad gents?" he asked.

"Nope," Tom said quickly. "I'm on for the fall roundup."

"You still carry a gun? Don't see you wearin' one now."

Tom wheeled around, feeling his cheeks turn hot.

"I hired on to swing a rope and that's *all*," he said, hoping to put the business to rest. "Any more damn questions?"

Bill looked down at his boots.

"Sorry, Mr. Spoon. Just curious. I never met a real shootist before."

Tom let his shoulders drop. "Ain't much different from any other man, son. Just the gun, and knowing how to use it. Call me Tom. No need to apologize."

"Sure thing, Tom. I won't bring it up again. It's just that a feller hears all those stories. Makes a man wonder."

Tom sauntered over and hung a hand on Bill's shoulder. "I'll tell you about it some time. Right now, my belly's rubbin' against my backbone. Show me to where we all get fed."

Bill grinned and some of the color returned to his face.

"Follow me. I'll lead you straight to some of the worst poison ever stirred across a plate. If you live past dinner, you'll be tough enough to make a hand at the Triangle Bar. We got ourselves a cook who milks a rattlesnake into every damn pot he puts on the stove. Bakes turtle-shell biscuits so hard they'll break off every tooth you've got before you can get 'em chewed."

"Lead the way," Tom said, taking a liking to the boy. "I was raised on rattlesnake milk and bedrock biscuits. I'm liable to like it here."

They crossed to a cook shack where a plume of smoke curled into the sky. Voices echoed from inside, until Tom and Bill came through the door, then everyone fell silent with eyes turned to watch the stranger, again. Tom followed Bill to a rough-cut plank table where they swung over a bench, seated with Slim and some of the others staring silently at Tom.

"Welcome to the Triangle Bar," Slim said, offering his hand. "I'm Dan Willis. The boys call me Slim. I'll introduce you around after we eat a bite."

"Much obliged," Tom said, feeling the heat of the eyes fastened on him. It was plain the gunfighter story had made the rounds. The looks they gave him spoke louder than words.

"Get yourself set for some dangerous chuck," Slim said when a potbellied gent came from the kitchen with a steaming pot, his face covered with greying whiskers. "This here's our cook. Calls himself Stewpot Smith, when he's in a good frame of mind. Me and some of the boys have got other names for him. When you taste what he's got in that pot, you're liable to come up with some names of your own for J.P. Smith. It's fair warning that Stewpot washes his feet in the same kettle he cooks in, so if your dinner reminds you of dirty socks, don't claim we didn't warn you."

The cook slammed his pot on the tabletop and glared around the room.

"I'd sooner slop hogs as to have the chore of feedin' this smartmouth bunch," he said. "Hog ain't got so much complaint."

The cowboy called Snuffy made a face and jerked his thumb toward the kitchen.

"I seen a few hogs back there only this morning," he said, as he began to ladle stew on his tin plate. "Spoke to one of 'em when I come to breakfast . . . thought it was ol' Stewpot. Looked about the same, 'cept for the whiskers. Must have been some of his kinfolks."

Stewpot wiped a hand on his greasy apron and directed his attention to Snuffy.

"It was a sow you saw, Snuffy. Same one you've been sleepin' with all summer. Heard tell you named her Rosie."

Stewpot shuffled toward the back, grinning through his untrimmed whiskers while the men passed pans of biscuits around the table behind the pot of stew. Tom took a helping of both and found the stew to his liking, no longer listening to the remarks made by the men while they ate, thankful that he was not the center of their attention for the moment.

When the meal was done he followed Bill outside. He shook hands with Snuffy and Sam and Lucky and Billy Bob and the rest, trying to remember names. It took no special talent to see the cautious looks the other hands gave him during the introductions, men who were wary of any stranger, not to mention a newcomer said to be a gunhand who had done a prison term for a killing. Tom had seen it before, written across the faces of men who knew him by reputation. Folks kept their distance.

Bill led him over to a corral where a group of young geldings grazed from a stack of hay.

"Take your pick, Tom," he said. "They'll be green broke, some better'n others. When you find the three you want, rope 'em and lead 'em to the barn. We saddle early around here, before sunup. The rest of today is yours, seein' as it's Sunday."

Tom gave the horses a careful look, finding a red roan he liked, then a bay and a black.

He knew some of the men were watching when he walked into the corral with a borrowed rope, to see if he knew his way around a lariat. He caught the roan on the first swing, then the others, settling the question. When the geldings were stalled in the barn he went off by himself to have a look around the place, since none of the men offered him much in the way of conversation.

He was first to roll out before dawn, first to the cook shack, first to pour coffee from the smoke-blackened coffee pot. The rest of the hands took pains to leave him sitting by himself when they came in for a plate of scrambled eggs, until Bill came over to sit beside him at a corner table.

"Mornin', Tom," he said sleepily.

Tom acknowledged the remark with a nod, blowing steam from his coffee. Stewpot came from the kitchen with a pan of biscuits for the early arrivals. He gave Tom a once-over when he slammed the pan on the tabletop, pausing before he went back to his kitchen.

"That was some ride you gave Big Blue yesterday," Stewpot said. "I've seen a goodly share of broncs rode in my day. Spent a year with the Goodnight outfit. Watched ol' Ben Cobb make his try on Midnight. Can't say as I ever saw a man better'n you aboard a bronc, Mr. Spoon."

"I'm obliged," Tom said. "He's one hell of a fine horse. Won't be many get the job done."

Stewpot agreed with a shake of his head.

"They've been tryin' 'round here for ten years. Nobody ever made it past the second jump. Jack could'a sold Blue to several of them rodeo outfits. Never would. That old stud must be close to fourteen. Maybe he's like the rest of us . . . gettin' old for the job."

Tom chuckled.

"By the way," Stewpot went on, "some of the boys say you're a quick-draw artist. You aim to lend Jack a hand with those owlhoots workin' for the railroad?"

Tom was less upset by the question than he had been yesterday. "Hired-on for the roundup . . . nothing else."

Stewpot wiped his fingers on his apron, frowning.

"Too bad. Ol' Jack could use some help this time. It ain't his nature to ask, but he ain't up to a match with the likes of Odell Pickett and his bunch. Could be you've heard of Pickett before. Mean hombre . . . a damn bounty hunter."

Tom felt his fingers tighten around his cup. "Seems I've heard the name," he said.

A moment from a distant past swept over Tom like a blanket. He saw himself taking measured steps to a spot where wagon ruts lay deep in the middle of an empty street lined with curious onlookers. Fifty yards away a tall, razor-thin gent spread his legs, his face shaded by a flat-brim hat. Then a hand made a move for the butt of a pistol, and Tom put his life on the line again. It happened a long time ago, before Tom Spoon knew what life would be like caged up like some wild animal.

"Take a word of advice," Stewpot said. "Keep an eye on your backside when you ride the south pastures. I reckon they told you . . . we've already lost two hands to a backshooter."

Tom nodded, and said, "I've been warned."

Stewpot left just as Slim came to the cook shack.

"Mornin', boys," Slim said, taking a seat and an empty cup. "Tom, you'll pair up with me. The boss wants us to check the waterhole at Comanche Springs . . . see if it'll hold through the summer."

Tom noticed Bill's face change before he spoke.

"Comanche Springs is south, Slim," Bill said.

Slim shook his head when his coffee was poured.

"There's four directions to ride on this ranch, Bill. One of 'em is damn sure south. The boss'll be proud to know one of his hands has got a sense of directions. I'll mention your name to him . . . give you credit for the idea."

"Just seems a mite hard on Tom, is all," Bill said.

Slim stared across the table at Bill.

"Wasn't a one of us hired to knit socks," he said. "There's horses in the south pastures, same as the others."

Slim helped himself to eggs and biscuits, dropping the matter, leaving Tom to his thoughts. They were riding to the region where the Triangle Bar hands were killed, to the water Jack Johnson wouldn't permit to be fenced off from his broodmares. Tom wondered idly if Johnson and Slim were testing his courage.

They were saddled before first light. Tom swung a leg over the red roan to follow Slim away from the barns. There was grumbling among the men, complaints about the early hour and low pay as the other hands scattered in pairs. One cowboy, the kid named Lucky, touched a spur to his sorrel and was promptly pitched over the gelding's head, sprawling to the dirt on his chest amid hoots of laughter from the men. The sorrel bucked to a stop near a corral fence while Lucky climbed to his feet and dusted himself off with his hat.

"Testing your wings, boy?" someone asked between fits of laughter.

Lucky socked his hat down over his ears and stepped aboard the gelding again, holding a tighter rein.

"Why don't we let Lucky ride Big Blue today?" someone else remarked, "now that Tom has broke him to a saddle. Maybe Mr. Spoon will give a few lessons."

Lucky ducked his head and rode off into the dark to escape the catcalls and hoots from the other riders. Slim chuckled and swung around to Tom, grinning a mouthful of teeth.

"When a man makes a mistake with this outfit, he gets more than his share of reminders," he said, then spurred to a lope down a wagon road leading south as the first grey streaks of dawn came to the sky.

They crossed gently rolling hills, toward a group of flat-topped mesas in the distance. The land was powder dry, bearing only scattered clumps of yellowed grass. Cactus grew everywhere, forming little knots of green amid the barren stretches of rock and caliche. Newly strung barbed wire ran fiddle-string tight down a fence row, somehow out of place across the hills.

Under his breath, Tom cussed the wire, supposing it was his age that made him hate fences. He had grown up in a time when the land was wide open, where a man could ride free in any direction without stopping to climb down and open a wire gap in a fence, or pull staples from posts to jump his bronc across. During the years he spent behind bars, Texas had changed, becoming a maze of barbed fences that scarred the land and turned it ugly. Fences always reminded him of a prison cell, where a small territory was declared to be the sole property of the man who occupied it, until another came along. Fencing land was no different. When the owner died or moved on, someone else came along to take his place.

It seemed unnatural, to claim ownership to a piece of

ground by enclosing it with barbed wire. Fences violated the laws of nature, holding some animals in and keeping others out. It was enough to make a preacher cuss, in Tom's opinion. But it was a sign of the times, proof that things had changed, and not to Tom's liking. Riding fenced land made him feel old and out of step with something called progress.

Two hours past sunup, Slim reined to a halt at the top of a rise, pointing down to a band of mares and colts grazing in a swale between two rocky hills.

"There's the Medicine Hat band," he said, pointing. "The boss likes that old spotted stud better'n any on the ranch. His colts are tougher'n bootleather, but hardly a cowboy in these parts can stand the color."

Tom watched the stallion grazing off to himself on a hilltop, a big black animal with a snow-white rump, like he was half of a black horse coupled in the middle with a white. If Tom hadn't known better, he would swear the horse was painted with a brush.

"Never saw such a thing," Tom said, taking note of the colts, some bearing the same coloration, white rumps glistening in the morning sun.

"Jack bought the stud from a trader . . . said he got him way up north in Indian country. Some folks call 'em a Paluse. Me, I call 'em ugly. Good horses, mind you, but I'd sooner be caught stealin' chickens than ridin' a two-colored horse."

Slim spurred off the rise at a trot, swinging wide around the band of mares, turning back for a word with Tom.

"The bossman calls the stud Chinook. Handle him careful if you're ever sent to bring him to the barns. He's Jack's favorite. Rather lose an arm than see any hide missing from Chinook."

They skirted the broodmares and left the wagon road to cross more of the same hills, holding an easy trot that would cover ground. Tom studied the mesas on both sides, deciding it was an easy place for an ambush; a rifleman easily could be hidden in the rocks.

With miles of ground to cover, Tom allowed himself some time to ponder the shape of things, the sudden turn of events that filled his pockets with money and brought him a job when he had all but given up on the idea. As he swept a look around at the empty hills, he was reminded of the longing he felt for so many painful years, waiting for the day when he would be free again to ride open country. With so much time, a dozen years, to think things over, he had had no doubts about the direction his life would take when he was free. There would be no more paydays with a gun tied around his waist, no more dead men to count or sleepless nights worrying about a backshooter or a bounty hunter on his trail. It was over, finished, done.

For too many years, more than he cared to count, Tom Spoon had lived on the edge, surviving only by his wits and his speed with a pistol. The balance of his life seemed too short to run those same risks again; besides, the prospect of another jail stretch was unthinkable to him now. He couldn't do it again . . . sit in a cell and have a little piece of his soul die every day. With whatever time he had left, he aimed to live free on the open range. He'd paid his debt. Unjustly, but it was paid anyway.

He remembered the day it all started. 'Ended,' was a better way to put it—the day he used his gun for the last time and found himself in front of a hand-picked Waco jury, charged with murder. There'd been a dozen witnesses to the affair, men who heard the other man challenge Tom to a gunfight over a hand of poker. Tom had done nothing more than oblige him, walking through the batwings to the street where he waited for his adversary's first move toward his gun. When the kid's hand clawed for his gunbutt, there'd been plenty of time for Tom to put a bullet into the mean-eyed boy. After it was over he'd gone back to the saloon to finish his whiskey. The shooting had been self-defense, plain and simple, with a street full of witnesses.

When the sheriff arrived, Tom had gone willingly to the jail to answer the sheriff's questions, never guessing he was walking into a trap. He had stepped into an office to find himself covered by shotguns, men who swore that it was Tom Spoon who called the other man out, and Tom Spoon who drew first with his six-gun. Weeks later, awaiting his trial for murder, he learned the identity of the kid—the son of the town's banker.

The boy fancied himself as quite a hand with the ladies in Waco dancehalls. He'd been losing to Tom at poker in front of his friends. Tom had been a stranger in town, enjoying some rest in a place where his reputation hadn't caught up with him. Not until Tom was behind bars did the Waco sheriff find out who they'd captured . . . Tom Spoon, a paid shootist with a reward on his head.

His trial was over in an eyeblink. He was found guilty of murder and sentenced to twenty-five years in state prison. All along, Tom remained convinced that someone would step forward to tell the jury the truth. No one did. And he'd had twelve years to think about it since.

Now Tom was determined to swing wide of the Triangle Bar troubles. He had seen enough of justice when it was bought and paid for. Jack Johnson would have to settle his own squabble the best he could. He would get no help from Tom, whose Colt was no longer for hire.

One dark thought gnawed away at Tom's brain . . . he hadn't counted on running across Odell Pickett. It was bitter medicine to have to turn his back on the likes of Pickett, but he would do it just the same.

Toward noon Slim and Tom entered deep canyons, as

rough as any Tom had ever seen. Slim swung his horse down a steep-walled ravine until it widened to a fork.

"This is the pass the railroad wants," Slim said. "It's the only way through the canyons for a locomotive. If they have to go around, it'll cost them better'n fifty miles of track. We lost two good men right here to drygulchers."

Tom studied the lay of the pass. A rider would be little more than target practice for a rifleman from the rim.

"Tough spot to ride through," he said. "Why doesn't Johnson keep his mares some place else?"

Slim grinned and shook his head.

"You don't know Jack Johnson, Tom. He won't tuck his tail and run from anybody. Besides, we need the grass, and you can't run livestock without water."

Slim urged his gelding to a trot, leading the way through the narrow pass. Now and then he glanced up at the rim. When they had crossed to the south side they rode up on the entrance to a box canyon where the ground was littered with horse sign. At the back of the little canyon sat a pocket of water, spread across a hollow in solid rock. The water was clear enough for a view of the bottom of the pool, an inviting sight for the men and the horses.

While the broncs drank their fill, Tom kept an eye on the rocky ledge around the top of the canyon.

"The spring'll hold," Slim said absently, after a study of the water's depth, "even if it don't rain."

"I ain't been asked," Tom began, "but if it was me I'd pull my horses off this range 'til the trouble with the railroad is over. There's liable to be some more good men killed. Makes it too easy for a shooter up on those rocks."

Slim nodded, squinting at the rim.

"Trouble is, this south end of the ranch has got the best winter grazing. If we pull the mares off, we'll have to buy feed 'til spring. Feed for better'n five hundred broodmares and colts—the cost would break Jack. Right now, he's a man caught between things . . . and his pride won't let him back off from the Texas and Pacific."

Slim turned to face Tom and gave a shrug.

"When you get to know Jack a little better," Slim said, "you'll understand. There ain't a man wearin' boots with more fairness in him. His handshake is his word on things. If he has a fault, it's his hard head to get things done his way, but he goes about it fair and square. His mind's made up on this railroad business. He aims to keep his land and use it the way he sees fit. Can't blame a feller much for such a temperament."

Slim reined away from the waterhole and started back through the pass, sweeping the canyon walls with a careful look until they were well north of the trouble spot. Tom did the same, wondering just how long it would be before some owlhoot was sent by Pickett to try to throw another scare into Jack Johnson. If Tom was any judge of men like Pickett, he figured it wouldn't be long. Drawing railroad pay to get the job done, likely with a track-laying crew sitting idle, some of Pickett's men would be sent to make another try in short order.

Slim struck a northwesterly direction and soon the canyons were behind them. Tom found horse tracks crossing the hills they rode through, recent hoofprints of mares and colts on bare spots between clumps of summer-dry grass. In an hour they sighted a fence row, running north to a wire gap where Slim swung down to lead his gelding through.

"Big place," Tom remarked while Slim stretched the gate back in place. "Somebody dug a hell of a bunch of postholes."

"You'll get your turn, Tom," he said, swinging a leg over his saddle. "Some of it's rock. If you ain't learned how to cuss quite yet, this place'll teach you how when you take up a posthole digger. One time I dug from sunup 'til dark on just one goddamn hole. Every time I ride past that post I give it another cussing. Had blisters all over my hands. When the boss talks about fencing off another pasture, there ain't a hand on the place who won't get down on his knees to beg him out of it. The good Lord didn't intend for a man to dig postholes in this country. Otherwise, He'd have made it softer."

Tom chuckled when he rode up beside Slim.

"I ain't much for fences in the first place," Tom said. "It don't seem a natural way."

They rode up on another herd of mares scattered over a group of low hills. Tom thought it a pretty sight, young foals grazing beside good mares or running free around the herd. It made him think all the more about wide open spaces, the way things should be.

A young stud bowed his neck and snorted at the riders, a glossy sorrel with a flaxen mane and tail, challenging the intruders in his domain.

"To my way of thinking, that's one beautiful sight," Tom said, trotting wide of the stallion's territory.

Slim reined in and sat to watch the herd.

"It damn sure is, Tom. Every now and then I cuss this job and wish I'd done something else with my life, but when I ride out here and see how things are, I'm mighty damn glad I made a cowboy. My pappy followed a pair of mules most all his life in a cotton patch. I always figured this was better'n looking at a mule's ass. I ain't made much money, but neither did my pappy. He died broke, which is what I'm liable to be, but I was never a prisoner to a plow handle."

Tom gazed toward the horizon.

"Bein' free to ride where you want is the most any man can have," he said gently.

Slim shook his head thoughtfully. "I reckon that's why I

stayed on to help ol' Jack fight the railroad," he said, staring off. "Never was much of a hand with a gun, but I aim to see this through. Times, a man's got to stand up for what he believes in. I sorta figure this ranch is my home."

Right off, Tom got set to offer an argument.

"Sometimes, it's better to ride away from trouble," he said, gathering his reins. "There's other places where a man can find ranch work."

"Could be," Slim replied, taking a quick glance Tom's way. "I suppose it depends on how hard a man will let another feller push him."

Slim rode off to put an end to the discussion, leaving Tom alone on the hilltop.

CHAPTER 3

HE was up before sunrise, struggling into worn boots as quietly as he could in the dark bunkhouse so as not to wake the rest of the hands. Outside, he stretched and rubbed sore muscles to take the stiffness away. A lantern glowed from the cook shack window. Stewpot was boiling coffee. Tom could smell it from the stovepipe above the roof.

Tom started toward the shack, then something stopped him in his tracks. Glancing up at the star-filled sky, he took a deep breath of fresh air.

"That's mighty nice," he said aloud, remembering other nights when he couldn't see the stars, a dozen years' worth, an eternity to a man like Tom Spoon. Twelve long years of prison, dreaming about a day such as this, a clean fresh morning without the stench of urine and sweat, without bars to confine him to a ten-foot square. "Mighty damn nice," Tom sighed.

His first night away from the prison had been the grandest of all, lying on his bedroll, gazing at the stars. He hadn't slept a wink all night, or even tried—he just savored the sights and smells free men took for granted. Listening to the call of a hoot owl in the distance, then the yipping cry of a coyote and the answer from its mate. Chirping crickets, the crackle of his tiny campfire, and the aroma of good strong coffee. Common things, but not behind prison walls.

"I won't go back," Tom said to himself. "Not for all the money there is. Not for any reason. I done my time. I sure as hell ain't gonna let no man shove me to a spot where I could do some more."

Tom started toward the shack, feeling better now that he'd said out loud what had been bothering him the day before. Slim's talk about the right and the wrong of things at the Triangle Bar and its troubles with the railroad had touched an old soft spot. A dozen years earlier, he'd have ridden over to that railroad camp for Jack Johnson's pay and called out Pickett. It would have suited him, then.

Siding with a man like Johnson against long odds wouldn't have required a second thought. Back then, before Tom became acquainted with the feel of chains around his bleeding ankles and the weight of a sledgehammer from dawn 'til dark, he would have felt totally justified in calling out Odell Pickett.

But twelve years in an iron box changed a great many things in Tom's life, decisions he made easily when he could saddle his horse and ride wherever he wanted. Locked away in a lonely cell, he'd had plenty of time to think about things. He decided then that his gunfighting days were over. Freedom was far more precious than any satisfaction he might get from avenging a wrong or defending a principle. A man could learn to swallow his pride and shut his ears to troubles.

Tom found Stewpot at his stove stirring dough for breakfast biscuits.

"Mornin', Tom," the cook said. "Coffee's ready. Help yourself."

Tom poured a scalding cup of coffee and blew the steam away from the rim.

"How was your first day on the Triangle Bar?" Stewpot asked, without looking up from his dough.

"Peaceful. I'm startin' to like it here already."

"Good outfit, Tom. Wasn't for them damn railroad troubles, we'd be sittin' pretty."

"Maybe it'll pass," Tom replied, wondering.

Stewpot shook his head.

"You ain't got to know Jack Johnson yet. He'd sooner lie down in pig shit than back off from his stand."

"Some men have got too much pride in 'em," Tom said.

Stewpot stopped his stirring and glanced at Tom.

"Pride's a funny thing, Tom," he said. "Too damn much of it makes a feller out to be a fool, but too little makes him a coward."

Tom shrugged off Stewpot's remark.

After breakfast Slim assigned Tom the task of helping Bill Hancock with topping off a string of young geldings. Tom was shown to a pole corral and given a bronc saddle.

"Take your pick," Bill said, thumbing toward a herd of horses in the next pen. "That big Palouse colt will be a handful. He damn near kicked the pocket off my pants when I tried to climb on his back yesterday. Watch him close, if you decide to take the Palouse."

Tom took a rope into the pen. The half-wild range colts swirled around him as he swung a loop. The big spotted colt made a run to the outside of the herd. Tom's noose settled over the colt's neck and the gelding snorted, whirling around to face the man who roped it.

"Easy, boy," Tom said, tightening the rope. "No sense fightin' me. We're gonna take it real slow."

Tom led the colt to the empty corral. It fought the rope when he snubbed the lariat around a fence post. Tom stood until the colt was convinced that the rope would not break, then he picked up the old saddle and moved slowly to the horse's left shoulder.

"Whoa, little man," Tom whispered, running his hand down the frightened colt's neck. Slowly, by degrees, the horse calmed enough so that Tom could fit the saddle across its withers.

Last, the breaking halter went over the gelding's nose. Tom kept talking to the colt, reassuring it with his voice and the gentle strokes of his hand.

He led the Palouse a few steps, until the hump was out of its back.

"See there. That saddle don't hurt a'tall," Tom chuckled.

A few minutes later he was aboard the young gelding's back, riding slow circles around the corral.

"I'll be damned," a voice said behind Tom.

Tom took his attention off the colt's ears just long enough to see who did the talking. Jack Johnson stood beside Bill Hancock at the fence, watching the affair.

"You're mighty handy with a horse, Tom," Jack said.

"Me an' this colt had a talk, before I swung a leg over him," Tom said, grinning. "I warned him that if he tried to kick me, I aimed to kick him right back."

Both men laughed. Then Bill went about his chores with the other colts, but Jack stayed at the fence, watching Tom for quite a while. When Tom pulled his saddle from the last bronc colt, Jack came over. It was plain he had something he wanted to say.

"You've got the softest hands on a colt's mouth I ever saw, Tom Spoon. Ain't many men got the touch, like you. Seems a damn shame you spent all those years behind bars. I wish I'd had you around to break my green colts."

Tom let out a sigh, gazing toward the horizon.

"Ain't no man alive any sorrier to be in jail than I was," Tom said. "A man don't miss his freedom 'til he ain't got any."

"Glad you signed on with us, Tom. You got a home here as long as you want."

Jack started for the main house. Tom watched him leave, thinking how glad he was just then to have stopped at the Triangle Bar to make his try aboard Big Blue.

Around noon the men ate a meal of cold beans and cornbread. Tom sat off to himself, more out of habit than any aversion to mingling with the other ranch hands. It had been a considerable spell since he'd had much in the way of mealtime conversation. In prison, he hadn't found anyone he wanted to exchange words with, anyway.

When his plate was tossed in the dishpan, he walked out to the corrals, leaning against a rail to watch the young horses. With a full belly and a job, and the fifty dollars stuck deep in his pant's pocket, Tom decided he was about as satisfied as he could remember being. Life on the run, before he went to prison, hadn't offered much in the way of contentment. Tom found that he was starting to like the ranching business. It suited him.

He topped off colts until sundown, then hung his saddle in the shed and washed for supper. Water from the rusty pumpjack felt cool on his face and hands. "I might just decide to take myself a bath right soon," he said, grinning at himself in the little piece of mirror hung above the wash basin. For a long time he had not cared to see himself in a mirror, or cared about taking baths, or wearing clean clothes. It was good to feel a little self-respect again, he decided.

Supper was beefsteak, Tom's first in many a moon. The longer he stayed at the Triangle Bar, the more he started to feel at home.

After supper he took a walk around the headquarters, filling his lungs with air, stopping now and then to gaze up at the stars.

"You're actin' a fool, Spoon," he commented to himself, "behavin' like a schoolgirl on a picnic, like you ain't never seen the sky before."

He started back toward the bunkhouse, scuffing his worn boots across the hard-packed ground, when a voice startled him.

"That you, Tom?" someone said.

Out of habit, his right hand fell to his side. Years ago his hand would have found the butt of his gun.

"It's me," Tom said, recognizing Jack Johnson beside an empty corral. "You spooked me. I figured I was all by my lonesome out here. Nice night, ain't it?"

Jack came over to him. Tom saw the grin on the rancher's face.

"I saw you reach for a gun just now, only you wasn't carryin' one," Jack said, chuckling. "Old habits are hard to break, ain't they?"

"I reckon," Tom replied sheepishly, scuffing a boot toe, "only, carrying a gun won't be a hard habit for me to break. I ain't gonna do it, plain as that."

"No need, long as you work for me, Tom," Jack said. "I meant what I said. You're hired for the fall roundup. A man who handles a horse like you, there ain't no call for him to wear a gun. You can earn yourself a living breakin' horses most any place on earth. You're smart to stay clear of trouble. If you can."

"That'll come natural for me from now on," Tom remarked, wondering about the change in the rancher. Two days back, he'd been trying to persuade Tom to hire on as a gunhand.

Jack started toward the house, then he stopped.

"Never had much envy for another man's ways, Tom, but I sure as hell envy your talent with horses. See you at daybreak."

Jack was out of earshot before Tom could think of anything to say.

Late one evening, Tom's third day on the ranch, Jack met him at the corrals when he rode in for supper. Before Tom swung to the ground he knew trouble was brewing, judging by the black look on Jack Johnson's face.

"Tom," he said, "come up to the house when you get your horse put away. Won't take but a minute."

Tom pulled his saddle, wondering. For days he had been about the ranch chores, enjoying himself doing simple tasks, repairing a windmill and tying up fence along the way, once roping a crippled colt to treat a stone bruise in its hoof. He was finding the peace he had dreamed about for so long. He had all but forgotten about the railroad and the Triangle Bar's troubles, off to himself on the ranch.

Tom trudged up to the house, spurs rattling over hard ground until he reached the porch, worrying about the meeting with the boss, expecting all manner of bad news.

Jack was seated in the front room when Tom let himself in the door, hat in hand. A lantern glowed on a nearby tabletop, spreading golden light over the room.

"Take a seat, Tom," Jack said. "Pour yourself a whiskey an' we'll talk."

Tom poured a shotglass and settled uneasily on the edge of a chair, waiting, watching Jack's face.

"Had some visitors today," Jack began, looking down at his folded hands, "officials from the railroad. Gent by the name of Carruthers, and a tall feller in a black suitcoat goes by the handle Odell Pickett. There's gonna be trouble, Tom. That's why I sent for you. Slim Willis tells me you've done a good job and I wanted you to know I appreciate it . . . an honest day's work for the pay. From here on out, the going's liable to get rough, so I'll pay your wages and you can clear out. I'm givin' every man on the place the same choices . . . stay an' be ready for a fight, or swing your loop for another outfit. I understand why you're stayin' wide of trouble, Tom. Another stretch in prison would be awful hard. This ain't your fight anyway, seein' as you hardly got your saddle hung in the shed. I know it ain't personal, but I've got to take a stand and you don't have a stake in this business."

Tom tossed down his whiskey and set the glass down.

"I know this fellow Pickett," Tom said. "If he's hired his gun to the Texas and Pacific, the men you've got won't stand a chance against him. He'll have a few with him, like as not, and they'll know their way around a gun. You're gonna get good men killed, Mr. Johnson. Pickett is a paid shootist, near 'bout as old as me. He's good . . . and real careful."

Jack let out a breath and frowned.

"I know you're right, Tom, but it don't change a thing," he said softly. "This is my land and I've always done with it as I saw fit. I'm too damn old to change. Comes a time when a man has to stand up and be counted. I'll face 'em alone if I have to, but I won't sell them a right-of-way. Slim has your wages for the work you gave me. Best of luck to you, Tom Spoon."

He stood up and offered Tom a handshake. Tom took the hand and turned away.

On the walk back to the bunk house Tom clamped his jaw and said nothing to the men lounging around the cook shack. He went to his bunk and rolled his worn blankets, then stuffed gear into his warbag, feeling the weight of the gunbelt at the bottom of the bag. Before he was done he heard the door close and tossed a look in that direction. Slim stood in the evening shadows with his thumbs hitched in his front pockets, watching Tom pack the last of his belongings.

"Clearin' out?" Slim asked needlessly.

Tom stiffened, angered by Slim's remark.

"You've got eyes," he said, jamming the warbag shut.

"No call to get riled, Tom. I was hopin' you would stay, is all."

Tom swung around, shouldering his belongings.

"It isn't my fight," he said softly, then he walked past Slim out the door.

He bridled his old dun gelding, the smooth-mouthed castoff he'd purchased with the four silver dollars that was given to every prisoner on the day of his release, the seed money to make a new start. Not many four-dollar horses could carry a rider very far, but he'd been lucky to find the dun among the cripples at the boneyard. Then he swung his worn saddle over the bronc, wrestling with his thoughts. The fact was he liked it at the Triangle Bar . . . liked the work and the other men and the bossman. Leaving went against the grain, but he had made himself a promise a thousand times over that he would never strap on a gun again. The state of Texas had given him years to think about it and his mind was made up. Tom Spoon could never do another stretch in prison. He'd as soon be dead.

He walked out of the barn into the fading shadows of twilight to find the men watching him. The same faces that had shown admiration a few days ago, after he rode the stud, betrayed disappointment in him— obviously the men figured Tom for a coward.

Slim approached him and handed him four silver dollars.

"Here's your pay, Tom. The boss called it a week."

Tom gave it back and shook his head.

"I didn't earn it," he said, glancing to the big house.

"How come you're runnin' out on us?" Bill Hancock asked, toeing a rock with his boot.

Tom let his shoulders sag before he answered.

"You wouldn't understand, son," he said. Suddenly, he felt the need to be sure Jack Johnson *did* understand. He started toward the top of the hill on tired feet, his mind made up to see the boss again before leaving, something his conscience demanded if he was to have any peace after he left the Triangle Bar.

He knocked on the front door, waiting, trying to figure what he would say. When Jack opened the door it was plain he was surprised to find Tom standing there.

"Come in, Tom," he said.

"No need, Mr. Johnson. Just wanted to explain best I know how."

"You don't owe me an explanation," Jack replied in a gentle voice.

"All the same, I aim to get it said. You already know I been to prison. Some men can't take bein' locked away, and I was one of 'em. Didn't know it 'til I got there, but when they put me in that cage I got my first taste of something I couldn't handle. First time in my life I was ever really scared of something. I spent twelve years in a box, starin' at walls, wishin' I was any place else—or dead. I couldn't do it again, Mr. Johnson, not for the best reason there is. I respect what you're doing against that railroad. If I could lend you a hand, I'd do it. I just plain can't. I hope you'll understand."

For a time Jack looked him up and down silently.

"Step inside a minute, Tom," he said, backing out of the way. "Take a seat and hear me out."

Tom walked to a chair, thinking it was Jack's play to try to talk him out of his decision. It wouldn't work, Tom knew, but he felt he owed it to Jack to listen.

"You've got guts, Tom Spoon," he said, removing a bottle from his cabinet. "For a man like me, it takes a hell of a lot more gumption to walk away from a fight than to roll up my sleeves and wade in. I admire you for it. Can't say as I'd be tough enough to do the same. Then, I ain't never been to prison. I know it changes a man."

Jack poured two glasses of whiskey and set one before Tom.

"My wife'll tell you I'm loaded down with faults," he went on. "Margaret says I'm stubborn as two green mules. Could be the woman's right. One thing I'm not guilty of is bein' shy of an opinion about things. The wife claims I've got one on most every subject, but there's one thing I know for sure. I'm of the opinion that nobody should be able to tell a man what to do with his own land. I've paid for thirty thousand acres with my own sweat and blood. Fought the damn Comanches and cattle rustlers and horse thieves to hold my claim. When some fancy-dressed gent from a railroad tells me I've got to sell him a right-of-way, it sticks in my craw like sand. Let 'em run their damn rails around my water. It's my land."

Jack knocked back his whiskey and made a face.

"So you see, Tom . . . I ain't got much choice. I've got to stand and fight that railroad just like I fought Indians. The railroad killed two of my men when I told 'em I wouldn't sell, and just today they brought out this feller Pickett, like I was supposed to be afraid of him. Well, I ain't. He may be better with a gun, but he ain't never tangled with Jack Johnson. There's more'n one way to skin a snake."

"Odell Pickett is a paid killer," Tom said, holding his glass of whiskey. "It won't matter to him how he gets the job done."

Jack agreed with a shake of his head.

"Could be, Tom. But I damn sure won't run from him. It figures I'll be fightin' the law and likely everyone else, but I aim to give it a try. Pickett's wearing a badge . . . calls himself a railroad detective. The Texas and Pacific has bought off our sheriff . . . even the Texas Rangers, but I'll tell you a thing or two about me . . . I was never one to worry about the odds."

Tom gave a sigh and emptied his glass.

"If things were different," Tom said softly, "I'd like nothing better than to side with you, but I can't help you."

Jack shook the notion away.

"I'm a right decent shot with a rifle," he said. "They don't

have me whipped just yet. Tell you what I'll do for you, Tom.
I've got a neighbor west of here who's in need of a good
hand, a widow by the name of Sara Clay. You ride over an'
tell her I sent you. She'll have some work. Pretty little woman,
to boot. Just follow my fence west 'til you come to the twin
mountains, then a half day down a wagon road. You'll like
Sara. It'll be an honest job through the winter."

"I'm obliged," Tom said as he came to his feet.

"I'll be doin' Sara a favor," Jack replied. "Best of luck, Tom.
Don't forget you'll always be welcome here."

They walked out on the porch to the cooler air of evening.
A soft summer breeze floated past, bearing a hint of dust.
Tom heard the jingle of spurs coming toward the house, a
man who was in something of a hurry.

Slim ran to the porch, out of breath. The light from a
window showed the worry spread across his face.

"They got Snuffy," Slim panted. "Billy Bob found him
along the fence east of the draw . . . got a bullet hole in his
belly. They brought him to the bunk house, boss. What'd
you want we should do?"

Jack's hands balled into fists.

"Goddamn them," Jack shouted. "Snuffy wasn't even carryin' a gun. Saddle some horses. We'll take a ride over to the
railroad camp . . . give the men the rifles."

Slim wheeled away from the house and trotted down the
hill. Before the sound of his boots faded, Jack was headed
for the front door.

"Don't carry guns," Tom said. "That's just what Pickett
wants you to do. He'll have an excuse to draw down on your
men."

Jack hesitated, reading Tom's face.

"I ain't takin' Pickett a basket of flowers," he snapped,

clenching his fists. "They killed one of my men. Snuffy's worked this spread for nigh onto twenty years."

Tom felt a knot forming in his belly.

"Leave the guns. I'll ride along with you," he said, wishing the words had stayed inside his mouth.

CHAPTER 4

SEVEN men rode behind the bossman to a bluff overlooking the sprawling rail camp. Fires burned across the flat prairie, red flames flickering between the white duck tents spread over a mile of equipment and material . . . stacks of rail ties and rusted iron rails, corrals full of harness mules, earth-leveling fresnos and countless wagons. Flatcars sat near the end of the rail line, loaded with more ties and rails and spikes. Singing and laughter floated in the night air. Tom guessed the camp would contain two hundred men . . . including the gandy dancers and whores who plied a living from the railroad payroll.

East of the camp, there was a pair of passenger cars, windows alight. That would be the camp headquarters, the likely spot to find Odell Pickett and his gunmen.

Jack spurred his horse off the bluff, followed by the Triangle Bar hands. Tom rode directly behind Jack, wondering why he had allowed himself to become a party to the confrontation with the railroad men. It was his own doing, to be sure, but the decision had been made in haste as he hoped to forestall more bloodshed. Now he realized there was no way to avoid trouble. Jack Johnson wasn't in the humor to conduct a friendly talk with the Texas and Pacific with a dead cowboy on his hands.

They skirted the campfires, riding around the tents to rein up at the two brightly lit passenger cars. Tom spotted the first trouble, two men slouched in the shadows beside pick-eted horses watching the eight horsemen approach.

A gent wrapped in twin gunbelts stepped out the back door of one railcar to survey the riders, his face hidden beneath a low hat brim.

"What's for you, boys?" the man asked when the horses were stilled beside the car, his voice deep, unfriendly.

"Tell your man Carruthers that Jack Johnson is here to see him," Jack said evenly. "Tell Pickett, too."

The gunman gave the men a careful look, taking note of the fact they wore no guns, then he turned into the car and passed a lantern-lit window on his way to the other end. Tom sat his horse, uneasy, risking a glance toward the two men in the shadows behind them.

The silence was broken by a horse stamping his hoof on the ground. Then the door of the car opened and a portly fellow came out wearing a silk vest and topcoat. He was followed by a tall shadowy figure Tom recognized even though the man's face was hidden below his hat brim. Odell Pickett gave the group a cautious look, one hand poised near the butt of his pistol.

"Carruthers," Jack snapped, "some of your henchmen killed one of my hands today . . . an old friend . . . rode for me twenty years. I'm here to hand you fair warning. We're done talking, you and me. The next shot that gets fired will start a war between the Triangle Bar and this railroad. Understand me, Carruthers. One more bullet crosses my land and there'll be hell to pay! Take my advice and run your rails around me. Hell'll freeze solid before I sell this outfit a right-of-way."

Pickett took a step toward the edge of the platform, still partially hidden by shadows, a fearsome silhouette under a night sky.

"That'll be a mistake, Johnson," Pickett warned in a low voice, hard to hear.

"Maybe so, Pickett," Jack replied, so casually it didn't seem they were discussing gunplay and death. "But I'm givin' you my word on it . . . one more shot and I'm comin' for this camp with guns. You can bet your bloody bankroll on it."

Pickett tensed, working the fingers of his gunhand.

"You're a dead man, Johnson," he whispered. "Bring your guns. It'll suit me."

Tom bit down hard, working the muscles in his jaw, then he touched a spur to his horse and rode closer to the platform.

"May not be quite that easy," Tom said, holding his temper the best he could, the light from one window spreading over his uplifted face. "Think on it some before you give it a try."

Pickett turned, just slightly, for a better look at the man who spoke to him. A heavy silence passed between them.

"Well, I'll be damned," Pickett said, one finger twitching on his gunhand.

"Been a long time, Odell," Tom replied, fixing Pickett with a stare.

The sounds of the rail camp swept past the railcar on a soft breeze. The two men glared at each other, until Carruthers twisted his neck toward Pickett.

"Who the hell is he?" Carruthers asked, irritated by the silence. Impatient.

"That's Tom Spoon," Pickett replied, a change in his tone.

"Never heard of him," Carruthers snapped.

Pickett paused, giving Tom a look before he spoke. "How come you ain't wearin' your gun, Tom?"

"No need of one yet, Odell," Tom replied. "Rather get it done another way, if you'll allow it."

"Pickett, why don't you do something? What the hell am I paying you for?" Carruthers asked, shouting loud enough to be heard around the camp.

It was Jack who reined his horse away first, wheeling his gelding before he spoke.

"You've had my warning, Carruthers," Jack said, then he stuck a spur to his horse's ribs and hit a lope away from the car. Tom held his bronc for a time, eyes fastened on Pickett as the rest of the men rode away.

"Be seein' you, Odell," he said, then he sent his horse to a trot behind the others into the darkness.

It was a silent ride over the twelve miles of dark ground to the Triangle Bar. Hardly a word was said among the hands until they swung down in front of the barn to unsaddle. The sight of Pickett and his gunmen had thrown a scare into the men, it was Tom's guess. Low-slung holsters and hard-faced shootists had put the affair in a different light among the Triangle Bar cowboys. It was one thing to talk about a fight with professional gunslingers, but another to face them when a war was about to be waged.

Jack turned to address the men when the saddles were hung and the broncs were put away.

"Boys . . . now you know what we're up against," he said. "If there's a man among you who wants out, I won't hold it hard against you."

Silent faces exchanged looks around the group. It was the kid called Lucky who spoke his mind first.

"Ain't any of us much with a gun, boss," he said, avoiding Jack's eyes, " 'cept for Tom, and you said he was leavin'.' "

Tom shifted his weight uneasily when he felt the stares of the men.

"Tom's riding over to the Widow Clay's place in the morning," Jack said. "He's got his reasons. Any of the rest can do the same. I'll draw up your wages in the morning."

Slim shook his head and took a step away from the group. "I'm stayin'. Count me in," he said.

One by one the men agreed to stay, some silently, some with a remark.

"Bill, load Snuffy's body in the wagon at sunup to haul him to the undertaker," Jack said. "He's got a sister in St. Louis. I'll post a letter to her. From here on every man on the place carries a rifle. Pair off and stay together when you check the pastures. I'll handle things if there's work to be done down around the springs. Get some shut-eye. Come mornin', keep an eye on your backsides."

The hands left for the walk to the bunk house. Only Tom stayed, until the rattle of spurs faded into the darkness.

"I owe you, Tom," Jack said. "Thanks for riding along."

Ever since they left the rail camp Tom had been torn by powerful emotions. Part of him wanted to stay and help the overmatched cowboys. If he ever had such a thing as a conscience, it was the voice inside his head that told him to throw in with Jack and the Triangle Bar men. When a man looked close enough he could usually find there was a right and a wrong side to things. Where Jack stood on the affair was right, plain and simple.

"You don't owe me a thing, Mr. Johnson," Tom said, sighing, wishing things could be different, staring off at the stars. "If I hadn't done those years . . ."

Tom's voice trailed off.

"I understand, Tom. Don't apologize. Best of luck with Sara Clay. Ride over here now and then. We'll drink up the rest of that Kentucky squeeze."

Jack stuck out his hand. Tom took it, but he found he couldn't look Jack in the eye.

CHAPTER 5

LONG before sunup Tom was saddled and ready to ride. He hadn't slept a wink all night, preferring the solitude of the barn to the bunk house. When he led the dun out of the stable he saw a shadow coming toward him, the unmistakable shape of Slim Willis walking bowlegged in Tom's direction.

"Had your coffee yet?" Slim asked.

Tom shook his head.

"I don't figure I'm welcome just now," Tom replied. "I reckon it'd be best if I ride out before the hands roll out."

Slim nodded, watching Tom's face. "There's some who don't understand. I figure it's your business."

Tom stuck a boot in a stirrup and swung a leg over his saddle.

"One thing's been bothering me all night," Slim said, rubbing his chin, thoughtful.

Tom waited, fingering his reins.

"When Pickett set eyes on you," Slim continued, "I'd swear an oath it scared him. Didn't seem he was so all-fired ready to ride rough- shod over the Triangle Bar."

Tom allowed a silence, then replied, "We chanced across each other . . . a long time ago."

Slim held Tom with a thoughtful stare, then he shrugged and stepped out of Tom's path.

"Be seein' you, Tom," he said, starting toward the cook shack.

He came to the twin mountains around noon, letting himself through the last wire gap marking Johnson land. A dim wagon road twisted through the hills to the west. He spurred the dun down the overgrown ruts, trying to shove the Triangle Bar mess from his mind.

After a couple of hours he came in sight of a crude cabin, set in the midst of scattered corrals where cattle bawled and dust swirled into a cloudless blue sky. A rider trotted through a pen of calves, swinging a loop for a catch, kicking dust into the air from the effort.

Tom rode up to the pens and sat, waiting for the rider to take notice of his arrival. When he looked closer, he saw that the rider was a woman, dressed in leather chaps and a floppy-brim hat, caked with caliche dust.

A moment later she saw him, after she'd missed a third loop intended for a brindled longhorn calf. Her face clouded, then she coiled her rope and rode to a gate where she swung down and tied off her horse.

He was surprised when he saw her face, expecting an older woman.

"What's your business, cowboy?" she asked. "I didn't hear you ride up."

"The name's Tom Spoon. Jack Johnson over at the Triangle Bar sent me. Said you needed a hand for the fall. I'm needin' work and it appears you've got some to be done."

She appraised him carefully, like some might size up a horse.

"I can't pay what Johnson pays," she said. "Ten a month and found. And a horse. Looks like yours has seen better days."

Tom chuckled, glancing down at the dun crowbait he rode.

"He's had a few too many years put on him," Tom agreed. "Could be I'm in the same shape, but I can still swing a rope and catch with it."

Her cheeks flushed suddenly and her green eyes flashed.

"I can catch," she replied hotly, "near good as any man."

Tom pulled off his hat by way of an apology.

"Wasn't about to imply you couldn't, Mrs. Clay. I miss a few from time to time myself."

She studied him again, making up her mind.

"What's your name?" she asked. "Didn't catch it the first time."

"Tom. Tom Spoon."

"Well, Mr. Spoon . . . the job's yours if you want it. If Jack sent you over, that'll be enough to satisfy me. Not many men will take orders from a woman. If you can handle it, strip your saddle and hang it in the shed. There's one other hand on the place, an old vaquero by the name of Luis. He's out just now to mend a windmill. I run ten sections of some of the roughest land in these parts. I'll give you fair warning . . . if you can't handle the work, I'll run you off. Don't figure because I'm a woman that I can't run a ranch."

"Such a thing never crossed my mind," Tom said, grinning before he replaced his hat. "Just tell me what you want done, Mrs. Clay."

"Call me Sara," she said, softer, some of the edge leaving her voice, wiping a sleeve across her face, a right pretty face Tom discovered. Her blond hair was tied back in a bun beneath her hat. Tom guessed her age to be middle-thirties.

Tom swung down and led the dun toward a ramshackle shed south of the cabin, deciding the place could use some repair, new corral poles in spots and some mending done to the barn. It had the look of neglect about it, the Clay ranch. A hammer and some nails were needed everywhere he looked.

Sara followed him, leading her bay, pulling oil-stained gloves from her hands. She was a small woman, upon closer examination, hardly the size of a stout corner post around her middle.

Tom pulled his saddle, smelling woodsmoke from the chimney of the cabin.

"I've got some stew," she said, still watching Tom with some caution. "You can wash up at the pump behind the house while I fix you a plate."

Tom hung his saddle and put the dun in an empty corral. Then he trudged toward the well where a rusted pumpjack sat above a circle of stones, the mortar fallen away in places around the top.

He filled a tin pan from the pump and rubbed cool water over his face and hands, knocking dust off his clothing with his hat before he entered the cabin. When he stepped on the porch a black cur dog growled at him, showing its teeth.

"Easy boy," he said, grinning down at the dog. "I'm a friend."

He pulled the latchstring and was met by a surprise. The front room of the cabin was as neat as a pin, decorated by a careful hand, unlike the shabby exterior of the place. His nose caught the smells from the kitchen, and his belly growled when he closed the door behind him.

Sara appeared from a room off the back with a steaming plate in her hands.

"Sit, Mr. Spoon," she said. "I'll pour you some coffee."

"If I'm to call you Sara, you ought to call me Tom," he said, sitting in a hide-bottom chair. He pushed a fork into the stew.

"While you feed yourself, Tom, I'll tell you a few things," she said, taking a chair opposite his, her face freshly scrubbed. "I run about three hundred cows on this spread. Longhorns. It'll be all we can do to keep them bunched. I've got no fences. My brand is the Circle C, on the left flank. Everything with my brand stays this side of the Concho. Late summer, the river gets low and I lose some strays. That's a part of the job, to keep Circle C cattle east of the river. It has been a dry year and the grass is getting thin. We'll have our hands full keeping my cattle on the place 'til the fall rains."

Tom nodded, eating with the best manners he could muster as she watched him.

"Tell me about yourself, Tom," she said after a minute of silence.

He swallowed, wondering just where to begin and how much he should tell Sara Clay.

"You already know Jack Johnson sent me," he began. "I had signed on with the Triangle Bar, but it looks like there'll be some trouble with the railroad."

"I heard," she said. "Jack lost two hands. The railroad wants a right-of-way through his land."

Tom stirred his stew, suddenly without appetite.

"I'm fresh from a prison stretch," Tom said, watching Sara's face closely. "I did my time and aim to stay away from trouble. If my past bothers you, I'll saddle and ride on."

Her eyes clouded briefly.

"I don't suppose it makes a difference," she said, "unless you handle a running iron better than you do a rope."

Tom shook his head.

"No, ma'am. I'm not a cattle thief. I reckon it's best to tell you straight from the beginning . . . I killed a man. I did a dozen years for it."

One slender hand paused near her face in the attempt to wipe a blond curl from her forehead.

"You're not wearing a gun," she said.

"No, ma'am. I'm finished with guns," he said.

Sara took a second look at him, more thorough than the first.

"I don't make it a rule to hold someone's past against him," she said. "If you do your job, I don't care what you did before you got here."

"That's about all a man could ask," he answered, finding he was uncomfortable when her eyes held him too long. "Mind if I ask a question?"

At first she hesitated, then she shrugged.

"How is it a woman takes on a job like this?"

Sara looked away. "This is all I have left, Tom. My husband died a few years ago. I have no place else to go."

"I'm sorry," he said. "Wasn't bein' nosy . . . just curious."

"It happens all the time," she replied in a tired voice. "Folks expect a man to be running the place, but I get by."

Tom cleaned his plate and drank the last of his coffee.

"Show me where to bunk," he said, climbing stiffly to his feet.

"You'll share the shed with Luis," she answered. "It's not very fancy."

Tom grinned and dropped his hat over his head. "It'll do. I'll unpack my gear, then you can show me what you want done around here."

When he walked out on the porch, the black dog snarled at him again.

"Quiet, Blackie," Sara snapped, shaking a finger.

Tom stepped wide of the dog and came off the porch.

"Show me the calves you want roped," he said, jerking a thumb toward the corrals. "It's my guess you want 'em made into steers, so I'll sharpen my knife and get on with it. Such ain't really women's work."

Sara's face darkened.

"Don't make any judgments about what a woman can do around here, Tom. You'll find out a woman can do most anything you can do, given the time and the necessity. You can rope the bull calves and castrate them when you're set in the shed. You may think it isn't women's work, but I'll lend you a hand if need be. I've done it by myself for a number of years."

Tom grinned again and shook his head. "I'll bet you have," he said, walking toward the shed. He hoisted his warbag over a shoulder and carried it inside to a sleeping room off to one side of the saddle shed. Three sagging cots sat along one wall, only one occupied with a man's bedroll. Cracks in the plank walls admitted sunlight, warning of what the shack would be like in winter. Deer antlers served as hatracks. A battered dresser sat crookedly in a corner.

"Home," he said to himself, tossing his gear on an empty bunk. He happened to glance at a shard of mirror hung above the dresser where a shaving pan sat beside a clean cloth. When he glimpsed the stubble on his chin he was reminded of how long it had been since he had been near bath water. His faded bib shirt hung loosely on his frame, wrinkled and stained, a poor fit after so many years of bad prison food.

He was suddenly conscious of the holes in his denims, and the run-over condition of his boots. His black flat brim hat had seen better days, drooped low in the front, stained by sweat and dust. He was forced to admit that he presented a sorry sight, something he would not have noticed had it not been for the woman and her pale green eyes and creamy soft skin. It seemed forever since he had worried about his appearance in front of a woman, deciding just then it was a foolish thought, given his age and all.

Even spruced up, he wouldn't make much of a suitor—a jailbird approaching his middle-fifties, a man with a dark past and no future. He didn't doubt Sara Clay would laugh at the notion of him considering fixing himself up to look more presentable. Likely, she wouldn't care if he wore tar and feathers, just so long as he did his job.

He took a last look at himself, at the grey hair hanging

down his neck in unkept curls and the grey stubble on his chin.

"A shaggy old dog, Spoon," he muttered before he walked out to the corrals.

He selected a decent rope from the saddle shed and swung his saddle over the dun, wondering about things . . . he'd need a better horse if Sara Clay aimed to have him cover much territory. And he wondered what the other cowboy at the ranch would be like, the vaquero she called Luis. As he rode toward the pen of calves, he took another look around the place, deciding after he'd done so that the little ranch suited him. He could make a home out of it, at least for one winter. And he had to admit to liking the woman's company, even though her raw beauty made him a bit self-conscious. It had been such a long time since he'd given any thought to women.

He rode through the pen, taking note of the recently cut calves still trailing blood over the dusty ground. The woman had done a crude job of it . . . too big a cut that left the steer a chance for swelling.

He swung a loop and caught the biggest of the bull calves, backing the dun to tighten the rope before he got down to do the job with his pocket knife. When he flanked the calf it let out a bawl, kicking, fighting the rope. Quickly he sliced open the skin and finished the affair, then removed the loop to allow the calf to stand.

"Nice work," Sara called out behind him. He had not known she was watching him.

He coiled his rope and stepped aboard the dun, blinking away the dust in his eyes, surprised to find a smile on the woman's face.

"Had lots of practice," he replied, suddenly aware of an odd tingle in his belly when he felt Sara's eyes on him. Damn it all, Spoon, he thought, you're carrying on like a kid at a church picnic. You're too old for such foolishness.

He swung another loop and flanked a second calf, making an effort not to look toward the fence where Sara stood. I wonder if she aims to stand there and watch me all afternoon, he thought.

By his guess she watched him about an hour, silently supervising the task as she leaned on a fence rail. The longer she stood, the more it bothered him, until finally she walked silently back to the cabin. He could not keep himself from watching her walk away, could not help the fact that his eyes fell admiringly to the sway of her hips in tight denims. When the cabin door closed he shook his head, hoping to clear it of young man's thoughts, and went back to the roping.

An hour before dark he looked up when he heard the click of horseshoes. A rider came from the north, his face shadowed by a trail-worn sombrero, sitting slump-shouldered on a grey.

"I reckon that's Luis," he said to himself, coiling his rope.

The vaquero rode to the saddle shed and stepped down, eyeing Tom warily. Then he reached down to pat the black dog when it came to greet him. The two men stared at each other briefly, then the Mexican stripped his saddle and disappeared into the shed.

Tom followed him into the shed, stepping wide of the growling dog.

"The name's Tom," he said, walking over to extend a hand to the Mexican. "I'm the new hand . . . signed on just today."

"I am Luis," he said, careful, suspicious. He took Tom's hand only briefly before he let it drop and went out to lead the grey toward an empty pen.

Not much of a beginning, Tom thought, watching the man. He guessed Luis to be close to seventy, his copper skin turned leathery by the sun, calloused hands that bore the scars of ranch work. Luis was tall for a Mexican and whipcord thin. He had shown his displeasure toward Tom right from the start. Odd, since a helping hand would make lighter work of the chores.

Tom put the dun away and walked to the pumpjack. Blackie followed along, snarling, showing his teeth, keeping a low growl in his chest while holding his distance. The dog and Luis made it plain Tom was not a welcome guest, leaving Tom to wonder what there was about him that Blackie and the vaquero didn't like.

He scrubbed his face and hands, then tossed out the water. His clothing was caked with dust and drying sweat following the afternoon of hot work in the dusty corral. He had blood on his shirtsleeves from the castrating and likely smelled like a billygoat; thus he made up his mind to apply soap and a razor to himself before supper with the dim hope of making his face more presentable. He filled the pan and carried it back to the shed. He found Luis sitting on his bunk, checking the loads in a pistol, one eye on Tom when he came through the door.

"You won't need the gun," Tom said. "I won't do the lady any harm."

Luis dropped the pistol back in a well-worn holster, a cutaway . . . the type of gear used by a man who drew a six-gun in a hurry. The gunbelt didn't fit the old Mexican, in Tom's view. Luis did not look the part of a shootist.

"I only use the *pistola* to kill snakes," Luis replied, tossing it beside him on the bunk. It was said in a voice that left Tom puzzling over the kind of snakes the old man was talking about. The kind that slithered along the ground or the ones that stood on two legs?

Tom lathered his chin from a shaving cup and applied his razor to his chin whiskers with his face to the piece of mirror. He could feel Luis watching him as he went about it.

When his chin was clean he passed the towel over his face and glanced at Luis. The old man had pulled off his sombrero to lean against the wall, staring at Tom. The light from a window played over the Mexican's bare skull. Not a strand of hair grew from his head, as bald as a slab of rock.

Luis looked like he might have been a muscular giant in his day. Age had taken away some of his strength, loosening the skin where muscle had slackened. His big hands looked powerful and Tom reckoned there would still be a job in store for anyone who made a try at wrestling Luis to the ground.

Tom wondered again about the gunbelt as he ran a hand through his tangled hair.

"How long you been working for Mrs. Clay?" Tom asked, to make a start at pleasant conversation.

"Many years," Luis replied softly. "Since I come up from Mexico . . . from Torreon."

Tom settled on his bunk, hoping for an end to the uncomfortable silence in the room. Luis said nothing.

The sounds from the wooden windmill filtered through the cracks in the wall, a creak of wind-driven blades and the rattle of a loose sucker rod. An uneasy minute passed, then two.

"Think I'll take a look around the place," Tom said when he could tolerate the silence no longer. "I'm a fair hand with a hammer and some nails. Maybe Sunday I'll see what I can do to help fix the loose boards around here."

He got up and walked out to face the growling dog again, feeling a cooler evening breeze on his skin. Smoke curled away from the cabin chimney, smelling of mesquite. Calves bawled in the pens, crying for the mother's milk they would do without after a few days of weaning. Tom took a deep breath of fresh air as he gazed around the ranch, enjoying the freedom and openness of being there. He would not allow Luis to spoil his enjoyment of the job, no matter what the Mexican's opinion of him might be. Doing the work was what mattered to Sara Clay—that, and minding his own business while he was at it. Time would take care of things on the Circle C. He would see to it, given the chance.

He took a stroll around the corrals, watching the shadows deepen with twilight until Sara called them to supper. Blackie snapped at his heels when Tom climbed the front porch, then the dog slunk away to a place near the steps, growling.

Luis came in and took a chair while Sara brought a bowl of beans to the table. Tom took a seat and waited until she joined the men at the table.

"I suppose you two have met?" she asked, directing her attention to Luis. "This is Tom Spoon. Tom did a good job with the calves today. Jack Johnson sent him over."

Luis merely shook his head, ladling beans onto his plate. Tom took a biscuit and started in to eat, mindful of his manners, wishing just then he had a clean shirt.

"Tomorrow I'll have Luis show you around the ranch . . . the boundaries . . . and the river," Sara said, applying butter to a biscuit with dainty fingers. "Give you two a chance to get to know each other. Luis has been with me a long time . . . since we built the place. He doesn't say much. Don't let it offend you, Tom."

At dawn they were saddled, Tom's gear tied on a bay colt Sara showed him in one corral, and Luis' aboard the grey. After a big breakfast of eggs and bacon they were off into the purple light of sunup, trotting west toward the Concho River that marked the edge of the Clay holdings. Luis had said nothing at breakfast, as silent as the day before, sweeping the land in front of them with a lingering look. A breeze came at them from the west, scented with dust, cool before the sun did its work.

Tom decided he would ignore the silence of Luis, give no more thought to it, or to the gun Luis wore around his waist tied low on his right leg. It did not matter that Luis wanted no conversation from him. Tom would not allow it to make a difference. Instead, he focused his attention on the land, the stretches of open hills and the distant mesas.

Yucca and cholla grew on the slopes among the grasses. Cactus were nestled in bright green clumps, budding yellow blooms. Quail darted from the path of the horses, spreading their wings for a low flight to the next hiding places.

Tom Spoon was a free man on this bright summer morning, a man without walls to hold him to a spot, free of the stench of men crowded together in cages, free to ride wherever he wanted. An empty dawn sky opened its arms to Tom, adrift with wonderful smells and sights he only imagined during those terrible years behind bars. Out here he could begin to forget about his past . . . the men who died in front of his gun. Strangely, when he thought about it just now it didn't seem a part of him, like it had happened to someone else.

They crossed a ridge where a herd of cattle grazed, an old bull lifting his head to watch them ride past, grass dangling from his muzzle, a six-foot spread of thick horns aimed to the sky. The Circle C brand ran across the flanks of the cows, scarred in the flesh of their multicolored hides. Luis hit a trot wide of the herd, skirting the bull's territory.

Before noon they came in sight of the river, a lazy brown current flowing southeast around rocks, twisting like a wandering snake across the land. On the far bank Tom spotted a group of cattle, tails tossed in the air as the riders approached, ready to make a run away from the horses.

Luis led down to the riverbank and sent the grey into the shallows. One mossy-horned longhorn cow snorted and flipped her horns at the men, then she turned tail and trotted off, leading the others. Luis spurred to a lope to ride around the bunch, whistling sharply between his teeth. Tom split the other direction, gathering the herd for a drive back across the river when he saw the Circle C brand.

One spotted cow bore a crude Bar Y brand on her right shoulder, a maverick that did not belong in the bunch. Tom built a loop in his rope and spurred the bay toward the river, gaining quickly on the spotted cow when she hit the shallow water.

He caught the cow by the horns and dallied the rope around his saddlehorn. The bay colt snorted and tried to down its head when the rope frightened it. Tom sawed back on the reins and hung a spur in the gelding's shoulder, just as the rope went tight with the weight of the spotted cow.

Just as Tom figured she would, the cow fought the rope, trying to follow the herd across the river. Tom reined the bay sharply, turning its tail to the cow, then he sunk both spurs into the gelding's ribs as hard as he could.

The colt leaned into the breast harness tied to the front of the saddle and lunged, jerking the cow off her feet. Tom spurred again, spooking the colt into a second lunge that pulled the longhorn over on her side on the muddy riverbank.

Again, he slammed the spurs into the bay. The cow scrambled to her feet, fighting the pull of the rope. Hooves fighting for a purchase, the gelding dragged the cow up the bank, too worried by the bits and the spurs to disobey the wishes of the rider.

A quarter mile from the river Tom slowed the bay colt and allowed some slack in the rope. He shook his loop off the wide set of horns and then drove the spotted cow over a hilltop, out of sight of the Circle C cattle. When he reined down on the bay the colt shivered, fearing the man and the rope until Tom ran a hand down the gelding's neck.

"Easy, son," Tom said, grinning. "You're a rope horse now. Nothing to be afraid of. This is how you're gonna earn your keep around here."

He hit a trot back to the river. Luis sat motionless on the grey, watching Tom approach until he was across the current and out on the other side.

"First time for the colt," Luis said. "I should have told you he don't know the lariat."

"Time he learned," Tom replied, coiling his rope, surprised by a remark from Luis, the first time he'd spoken all morning.

"You a pretty good *caballero*," Luis offered before he reined away from the river. "Maybeso you be okay."

They rode up a swell to a piece of level ground, watching the bunch of Circle C cattle move away from the river. Luis ran a hand over his face, then he pointed to a set of hills to the north.

"We go this way, Tom Spoon," he said. "Maybeso find some calves to drive back to the corrals for the knife."

It was the most Luis had said to him since he had come to the ranch, a start, a sign things might not go so badly after all, working for Sara Clay.

CHAPTER 6

IT wasn't much, he decided, reflecting on last night's change in the way old Luis regarded him . . . a few words of conversation and a gentler look in his eyes following supper. It was a beginning that held better prospects for a winter spent in the same tiny room with Luis.

Tom crested a butte around noon near the east fence, the Triangle Bar fence that held Clay cattle off Johnson range, and spotted the windmill standing on a hilltop beside a stone trough, its blades turning in a slow breeze. He headed down the slope for a check of the water, like Sara wanted, a weekly chore on the Circle C where water from the wells was so vital.

When he rode up he sighted trouble right off at the top of the tower . . . the brake had worked itself loose, hanging crookedly away from the shaft, useless. Tom got down and tied off the bay, preparing for a climb up the wooden tower.

With tools in his back pocket he scaled the weathered boards, careful to avoid the blades, climbing with his face to the wind. A bolt had fallen from a bracket that held the brake in place, a simple repair with the right tools and a new bolt.

While he was about the task he swept a look at the land now and then, sighting a small herd of cows ambling toward the water trough, walking along the fence. From the tower he had a fine view of Clay land, the hills and mesas, the twin mountains and a crisp blue sky. The more he settled in to life at the Circle C the better it suited him. And there was Sara Clay and the way her beauty had begun to stray into his thoughts more often, on the long rides across the ranch, and at night when he lay on his bunk ready for sleep. He realized that he was often thinking about her and his chances at sharing her company, a wild flight of fancy to be sure, but still tugging at the corners of his brain. If it was nothing else, it was a pleasant way to pass some idle time.

When the cattle reached the water, they approached him with snorts of caution, unwilling to risk a drink with a two-legged beast hanging from the tower above the trough. When the bolt was tightened in place, he pocketed the wrench and started down, until his eyes fell on a brand burned across a cow's hide, a Triangle Bar.

"Johnson's cows," he thought. "Fence must be down."

He climbed to the ground and rode off a distance to allow the herd a drink, then he rode around the bunch to start them back along the fence, looking for a hole or a missing staple where the cows had pushed through.

He wasn't long finding the trouble. In a draw less than a mile from the windmill he rode up on loose wires, then a spot between fence post where three strands lay curled on the ground. He pushed the cattle through the hole and swung down to examine the fence. The barbed wire had been cut cleanly with a fence cutter. When he walked around the spot he quickly found the tracks of two shod horses.

For a time he studied the ground, reading the sign.

"It isn't the work of a Triangle Bar hand," he said to himself. "They've got more grass on their side of the fence than Sara, overgrazing like she does. This is somebody out to cause Johnson trouble . . . scatter his cattle and make fence work for his hands."

He set about to stretch the wires, mending the cuts with a small spool of bare wire he carried in his saddlebags, giving more and more thought to the damage done. It was likely another effort from the railroad bunch, dealing Johnson

enough misery so he'd think more about the right-of-way. If
fences were cut all over the Johnson spread, it would take an
army of men to piece the wires back together and round up
the cattle and horses. It was a plan that stood some chance of
success against most men . . . unlikely to change Johnson's
mind if Tom knew the man at all.

When the fence was tight he mounted and started back
for the ranch, wondering about Slim and Bill and Lucky and
the rest, hoping the gunplay was ended—but knowing better.
Odell Pickett was out to earn his money and Jack Johnson
wouldn't back off from his stand. It wouldn't end with a few
cut fences. Pickett would see to it that more blood was spilled.

A short distance from the fence he reined down suddenly
to study sets of hoofprints. Two horses had ridden west across
the hills. For a time Tom sat, unable to figure why two men
would cross Sara Clay's land. It could have been the same
pair who cut the fence . . . about the same tracks, the size
and shape of the hoof.

He set out along the prints, puzzled, aimed due west. In
an hour the direction had not changed, cutting across open
land in the general direction of the Circle C.

Another hour brought him to a rise above the ranch where
the hoofprints stopped. Another puzzle, then the men had
turned north.

Getting the lay of things . . . maybe, he thought, unable to
figure the purpose behind the tracks. Someone had ridden
to a vantage point above the cabin, stopping long enough to
leave horse droppings while they looked over the place. It
didn't make much sense. Sara Clay's holdings weren't a part
of the land the railroad wanted.

Following a hunch, he rode the tracks 'til dark, north of
the dry creekbed marking the boundary of the Circle C
where he and Luis had gathered a handful of calves the day
before. In the twilight Tom noted the northward direction

of the two horses aimed for a little town Luis described, on the far side of a group of mountains, a place called Knickerbocker. Perhaps the hoofprints were nothing more than a couple of drifters who cut the fence on their way across country. It didn't figure that they could be railroad men . . . not so far west of the Triangle Bar.

He hurried the bay toward the ranch, wondering about the tracks. Then he thought about other things, the way Sara would look at supper, and the way her eyes smiled, wrinkling at the corners when she looked at him.

He was late for their meal and gave his apology.

"I found a hole in the east fence," he said, cutting into a steak while Sara and Luis sipped coffee. "I fixed the windmill and found some Johnson cattle coming to water."

Sara seemed unconcerned, at first.

"The wires had been cut," he said. "I drove the cows back and mended the cut. Followed two shod horses west to the hill above the ranch. Who ever it was made a stop, looking things over, then they rode north, toward Knickerbocker."

Sara's face went dark.

"Who would cut our fence?" she asked Luis.

Luis spent a moment deciding, watching Tom, then Sara.

"Quien sabe?" he said with a shrug. "Maybeso it is nothing."

Tom glanced toward Sara and was reminded of his manners. She wore a soft white blouse instead of the man's shirt of yesterday, and allowed her golden hair to fall freely down her neck. In the lantern light she seemed even more beautiful than before, more womanly, stirring feelings in Tom's chest he wanted to ignore . . . if he could.

"I suppose we can keep a closer eye on the east fence," she said, "check it twice a week, now that we've got another hand around the place. It's the river that worries me. We haven't had a rain in a month. It'll be harder than ever to keep the cattle where they belong."

"Hardly more than a trickle," Tom replied, remembering the shallow crossing where he had roped the spotted cow.

"Well, I can do my share," she said. "Tomorrow I'll saddle a horse and make a swing along the Concho. With Tom around, I started to get lazy."

She gave Tom a grin that sent a flutter into his stomach. He felt his cheeks turn hot and felt like a girl after her first kiss.

"Luis and I can get things done," he said. "No need to hit your saddle, Mrs. Clay."

"Call me Sara," she said, softly, making his flush seem worse.

"Yes ma'am. Sara it is," he said, forcing his eyes down to his plate so she wouldn't notice.

After supper he and Sara walked out on the porch under a sky filled with stars. A cooling breeze came from the west, reminding Tom that he should stay downwind until he could wash his other shirt and take a bar of soap to himself.

"I think I'll take a bath," he said, "now that it's dark. If you'll excuse, me, Mrs. . . . . Sara, I'd better see if I've got a clean change."

She smiled at him and he wondered if she was teasing him with it.

"You can pile your clothes on the back porch, Tom. In the morning I'll wash them with the rest."

"I'd be obliged," he said, tipping his hat. "It's been a while. You might want to soak 'em first."

He stepped off the porch and clumped through the dark, his mind wandering, considering the chances that Sara might think of him as something other than a ranch hand. It was an absurd notion to think that a woman so young would take a fancy to an old jailbird cowboy like himself, but he thought about it anyway. So many years had passed since he'd had a woman that the prospects frightened him a little. He wouldn't remember what to say, or how to act, or any of the proper things. Given the chance, he would likely make a fool of himself, which was no different than figuring Sara could take a shine to him in the first place.

He carried his change of clothes to the pump and took a quick look around, to be sure Sara wasn't watching. Then he shucked off his boots and denims, and last his shirt, standing naked in the starlight with a bar of lye soap in his hand. Blackie growled from a shadow beside the porch, probably a comment about Tom's unsightly nakedness.

"Quiet, dog," he said. "This is bad enough without an audience. Keep your opinion to yourself."

He pumped cool water in the pan and began the chore of soaping himself, flinching when the water brought goose-flesh to his skin. The scented soap made him feel all the more a fool, but smelling of perfume like some dancehall whore was decidedly better than a cowboy's natural odor.

Shivering, he dowsed himself with the water in the pan and made a cursory swipe with the towel to dry himself off. Blackie snarled again and came creeping from the shadows, showing Tom a mouthful of teeth. Tom glanced toward a lantern-lit window at the back of the cabin and saw move-ment behind one lacy curtain. Reflexively, he covered himself with a hand and blinked, trying to be certain of what he saw.

Wonder if she's been watching me, he thought, grinning when he imagined it, then he shook the idea away. "Not much to see 'cept a skinny old man, white as a bedsheet where his skin don't get the sun," he muttered to himself.

He pulled on his pants and then his socks before he forced his feet into his boots. Once, he took a look at the window again. He couldn't be sure, but he thought he saw the curtain flutter. It could have been only a current of air.

"I will ride north," Luis said, tightening his cinch. "You ride the river. I will come east. The grass is bad north and there will be only a few cows. I will help you when I ride along the river from the north."

Tom swung up and rode away from the shed in the first false light of dawn. The bay colt was settling down to make a good ranch horse and his gait was easy, making for a softer time in the saddle.

When daylight came Tom spurred to a lope, following a trail toward the river. During the night he had tossed and turned on the cot, dreaming vague dreams about Sara and women in general, which was a topic he was forced to avoid over the years. It was unsettling to find that a woman's face began to haunt him in such a fashion, floating before his eyes when his mind was vacant, stirring old emotions he thought almost forgotten. The longer he looked at Sara Clay, the more she bothered him. It had begun to seem she was dressing *for him,* making the effort to be more feminine, leaving her hair down and smiling more often. It could have been the work of imagination. For the moment, Tom couldn't be sure.

He rode up on the river and saw cattle spread over the far bank, grazing the thicker grasses. The shallow Concho did little to discourage a hungry cow. It would fast become a full-time job to hold the cattle on the Circle C range unless it rained.

He crossed on the bay and drove a sweep around the longhorns, slapping his rope against his leg, spooking the wild cows into a run back across the water. The chore consumed most of the morning, until the last Clay cow was where it belonged.

He glanced toward the sky . . . cloudless, with no prospects of rain.

It'll be a dry fall, he thought, remembering other years that had begun in a similar fashion. With too many cattle to support, Sara's ranch would have a hard time of it without rain.

He rode north along the river, planning to meet up with Luis on his swing down from the north boundary. When his mind was idle he thought of Sara again, until he caught himself.

"You've made yourself plumb loco over a woman," he told himself, "gone crazy in your old age."

In spite of the admonition, he formed a plan to ride over to Knickerbocker in the morning, to buy a couple of new shirts, some good denims, maybe even a hat with part of the fifty dollars he'd won riding the grey. "No reason a man shouldn't look respectable. And tomorrow is Saturday, anyway," he said to himself.

He sighted Luis coming at a jog down the river and shook off the thoughts about the woman. When he rode up beside the vaquero the old man actually grinned, like he was glad to see him.

Supper was a fancy affair. A big apple pie sat in the middle of the table, smelling sweetly of cinnamon. Sara's face was scrubbed to a nice pink, and her hair was brushed and combed with a piece of green ribbon tied for a gathering, matching her eyes. Tom's belly had begun to flutter long before they sat down to eat . . . he couldn't be sure if it was the pie, or the woman that made his insides jump.

"Thought I'd ride over to Knickerbocker in the morning," he said, trying to sound casual about it. "Been a while since I fixed myself up with new duds. My outfit looks a little trailworn . . . and I'll need a coat for the winter so I don't freeze solid."

He couldn't be sure, but he thought he noticed a look pass over Sara's face, a look of approval.

It was his first piece of apple pie in over a decade, perhaps that was one reason it tasted so good. He cut small hunks with his fork and tried to eat like a civilized man should. Manners were another thing he hadn't been accustomed to for a very long time. There'd been no need until now.

CHAPTER 7

IT was a pleasant ride that took three-quarters of the day before he reached the tiny town of Knickerbocker. One giant building occupied the town square, surrounded by several small stores, a pair of saloons, and a building that obviously was a court house where county government was conducted. Tom rode to a hitchrail and tied off in front of a mercantile, admiring the flowing dresses of the women who paraded along the boardwalks, sunbonnets ribbon-tied to shield their faces from a blistering sun.

The store was a marvel to behold, rows of shelves filled with all manner of goods. Too many smells came at him at once for him to be able to properly identify more than one or two, scented soaps and hair tonics mingled with the clean scent of new cloth.

He worked his way to the back, to shelves of clothing, stopping now and then to admire this or that, touching a thing with his fingers when it struck his fancy. After so long without it, shopping was giving him great pleasure, like it had when he was just a boy hanging on to his mother's skirt.

After much deliberation he bought two bib-front shirts, a deep blue and a soft brown. Then two tight-fitted denims and new socks and a split-tail duster coat lined with wool. Good beaver hats were too expensive . . . ten dollars for the one he fancied most. Thus he decided against the hat and added a bottle of rose-scented hair tonic to his purchases. Then in a moment of silliness he bought a bottle of perfumed water for Sara, since it would be Christmas soon enough and he would need a gift for the occasion. He even bought a red bandana for Luis. He left with a twenty-six-dollar bundle he carried under his arm and tied behind his saddle for the ride back to the ranch.

His belly growled as he rode past a lantern-lit saloon on his way out of town. He reined over to a rail where eight or nine broncs stood hipshot in the dusk of evening. His plan was to buy a bottle of whiskey for the cold winter nights, and to eat from the free cracker barrel most drinking parlors kept for their customers. When he walked inside he cast a quick look around the patrons, a habit from his past where it paid to know who would be behind him. When his glance passed over the men at the bar he realized his mistake, too late to make a turn back for the batwing doors without notice.

Two gunmen from the railroad camp slouched against the long wooden bar, their eyes on him as he walked up to the barkeeper. One was the gent who wore two pistols Jack spoke to when they rode up on the rail car. Tom did his best to be casual about his arrival in the place, leaning elbows on the polished wood before he spoke to the barman.

"I need a bottle of whiskey," Tom said softly, digging some silver from his pocket. "I'll take it with me."

From the corner of his eye he saw the pair watching him with interest. With his hat pulled low there was a chance they wouldn't recognize him before he paid for the whiskey and got clear of the place.

"You men pay attention," one of the gunmen said, addressing the room in a voice loud enough to halt conversation. "We've got a famous feller among us. I'd say we're honored by him just now. Have a look over there at the bar at Mr. Tom Spoon. Talk is, he made quite a name for himself with a six-shooter. I reckon some of you have heard of Mr. Spoon.

Let's all pay him his due and drink to our new guest. Here's to Tom Spoon," he said, raising his glass.

Tom clamped his jaw and gave momentary thought to what he knew would follow. The pair wouldn't leave it alone, judging by the whiskey-thick voice and the sullen looks they gave him. There would be more, until they could goad Tom into a fight or make him crawl out of the saloon on his belly.

He tried to ignore the remarks, knowing it would not work but determined to make the try.

Then he heard the rattle of spurs on the floorboards, coming in his direction.

"How come you ain't wearin' a gun, Spoon?" the gunman asked, surly about it, taunting him with the tone of his voice when he stood near Tom's shoulder.

"No need," Tom replied, turning just a little for a look at the man who spoke.

He was young, early twenties perhaps, with the look Tom had seen so often on the faces of men who fancied their talents with a gun. Most were arrogant, sure of themselves until a bullet wiped the haughty look from their eyes. More than once, Tom stood over the body of a man whose blood pooled around the spot where he lay, his life ebbing away, his face showing a look of surprise that Tom had beat him to the draw. There was no way to educate their kind beforehand. Nothing short of a bullet hole made them understand how wrong they were about their skill.

"Could be there's need now," the gunman said, grinning crookedly. "If someone was to call you out just now, I'd say you oughta have a gun."

Tom shook his head and turned back to the bar. "I don't carry a gun anymore, son. Why don't you leave it alone."

With the words fresh from his mouth, Tom knew it was a waste.

"Maybe you've gone yellow, old man?" he said. "Maybe you're too damn old to handle the likes of me?"

Tom closed his eyes briefly, wishing he was some place else.

"I'm not lookin' for a fight," he said. "Just wanted a bottle of whiskey."

The man chuckled and swung a look toward his partner.

"Maybe Mr. Tom Spoon is just an old drunk these days?" he said, then he turned back and took a step closer. "I'm callin' you out, Spoon. Go get your gun. I aim to see if Odell is right about you."

Tom sighed and paid for the whiskey the barkeep placed on the counter, two silver dollars rattling in the heavy silence of the barroom.

"I don't carry a gun," Tom said, fisting his jug to walk away from the trouble.

It came from Tom's blind side, behind him, a big-knuckled fist swung across his ear. He was knocked spinning away from the bar by the blow, losing the bottle he held when his feet went out from under him.

He landed on the floor and lost his hat. When he tried to scramble to his knees a boot toe slammed into his ribs, sending him rolling under a nearby table, scattering chairs. Pain shot through his chest, then a boot smashed into his face and he tasted blood.

"Get up, you old bastard," the man cried. "Crawl out to your horse and get your damn gun."

Stars flashed across Tom's vision. He tried to crawl out from under the table and was kicked again, knocking him over on his back. Suddenly he couldn't breathe, too dizzy to stand or get his senses.

"I say Tom Spoon is a goddamn coward," the gunman shouted. "He's too old to get up off the goddamn floor. Just take a look at our famous guest, boys. He's down on his hands and knees like a drunk Injun."

Tom rolled over painfully to his belly and got a breath. Blood poured from his mouth, dribbling on the floor, smelling of copper. Slowly, shaking with the effort, he pushed up on his knees and grabbed a chair to steady himself.

"Take a look, boys," the gunman snarled, standing over Tom. "Take a look at the bigshot gunfighter, Tom Spoon. I say he's washed-up . . . done for. Ain't nothin' but an old saloon drunk."

Some of the patrons chuckled . . . Tom heard them as he came slowly to his feet, swaying. Then he bent over and picked up his hat, holding on to the chair, before he walked unsteadily to the batwing doors without a word.

He spit blood and untied his reins, trying to hold a stirrup so he could mount the bay. It was a painful pull over his saddle, then he reined away from the saloon.

He rode out of Knickerbocker at a walk, unable to tolerate the jolting gait of a trot with painful ribs. When he was clear of town he put fingers to his mouth, feeling the lumpy flesh where the boot had struck him. There was a swelling above his left eye that threatened to close it, painful to the touch, throbbing with the motion of the horse. He wondered if his ribs were broken. It hurt to take a deep breath.

An hour away from town he felt better. The dizzyness left his skull and he was able to keep his mind on the direction he took.

Several hours before dawn he rode down to the ranch and quietly put his gelding away. He crept into the shed, so as not to awaken Luis, then he fell asleep across the bunk.

"Madre," Luis said, an exclamation of surprise as he stared down at Tom's face. "You hurt, Tom?"

Tom blinked open his eyes and sat up. Sunlight poured through a window, hurting his eyes.

"Yeah, I'm hurt, Luis," he said. "Mostly my pride. I met up with a couple of gents in Knickerbocker. I'll live."

"Like me, you are too old to fight," he said softly. "I will bring some water from the well so you can clean the blood off your face."

Luis carried the tin washbasin out while Tom took stock of his injuries, hobbling stiffly to the mirror, holding his painful ribs. The reflection he saw was barely recognizable, one eye swollen shut, dried blood around his mouth, down his neck to his shirtfront. He tried to force a grin, for a pair of reasons, to see if all his teeth remained, the other to laugh at himself for the shape he was in.

"Damn it, Spoon," he said to himself, "you've gone and made a mess."

He limped back to his bunk and sat, careful to move slowly as Luis entered with the water and a cloth. With the washpan beside him he began gingerly to wipe the blood away, wincing when the rag touched his lumpy cheek and lips.

"Who were these men?" Luis asked, watching Tom minister his wounds.

"Couple of gunhands workin' for the railroad. They saw me ride up to the rail camp with Jack Johnson . . . recognized me, and tried to push me into a gunfight."

"You do not carry a *pistola*," Luis said.

Tom nodded tiredly, dipping the cloth in the pan.

"Did once. Some folks ain't inclined to forget."

"Sara told me. You killed an *hombre* and went to prison."

Tom sighed, and the act pained his sore chest.

"Killed more than one, Luis. It was a long time ago."

Luis took the pan when Tom was finished and tossed the water out the door.

"Sara will have breakfast now," he said.

Tom shook the idea off and lay back on his bunk.

"Tell her I ain't feelin' well today. It's the truth. I think I'll skip the food."

Luis walked out. When the door was shut Tom allowed himself a moment to think back over things. He was proud of being able to walk away from a fight, and to suffer the attack without being tempted to get a gun. To put it more accurately, he had crawled away from the fight, but he was still a free man without leaving a killing in his wake. He had kept his word to himself, by backing down at the saloon as well as by riding away from the Triangle Bar troubles. Could be he *was* a changed man.

When he closed his eyes he saw the face of the young gunman leering at him from last night's scrape, heard the challenge in his voice, remembering what it was like to take the punishment. Times certainly had changed for Tom Spoon. A reflex, his hands closed into angry fists, then he relaxed them quickly. It would do no good to let his blood boil over it. It was done.

He heard the door open and opened his eyes to find Sara beside his bed.

"Oh, Tom," she cried softly. "Luis told me what happened."

"I'll heal," he said, wishing she had not come to see him like this.

"I've got some salve in the house. I'll be right back."

She was gone before he could offer protest. One thing he didn't need just now was mothering. He didn't want her to see him looking like a piece of raw meat at butchering time.

She returned and sat beside him, tenderly rubbing pungent salve on his wounded face. When he gazed up at her he noticed her soft hair, and the gentle looks she gave him. Something stirred inside his chest.

"When I get up and around I'll nail a few boards around

the place," he said. "Winter'll be here before we know it and then it'll be too cold to get it done."

She nodded and stood up, then she gave him a soft smile.

"I'll bring you a bite to eat," she said, turning for the door.

"That'd be a waste," he replied, trying to form a grin. "I don't figure I can open this mouth wide enough to shovel it in."

She left him alone with his thoughts, to sort through the odd feelings in the pit of his stomach, not from the beating but from the nearness of her. The woman affected him so much that one look at her face filled his head with crazy notions.

Later in the morning, she brought him coffee and biscuits. He discovered he had no appetite until she left the shed. He ate sparingly and drank the coffee slowly.

It was noon before he could get around well enough to find the hammer and some nails. Bending over was like taking a hot branding iron to his ribs, unless he went about it slowly. He nailed down some loose boards around the shed, limping to get from one spot to the next. Luis threw in to help with the corral poles, silent for the first couple of hours, until the heat of midday drove them to the shade for a rest and a dipper of water.

Luis stared off toward the hills for a time, then he fixed his eyes on Tom.

"Many years ago," he began softly, "I called myself a *pistolero*. I, too, have killed men with my gun. I joined the revolution when I was only a *niño* . . . fifteen *años*. In Torreon, I became *malo hombre*, a bad one. I did not count the ones I killed."

He looked down at his boots, then he went on.

"At Sabinas, when I was much older, I came to a cantina where the most famous of all *pistoleros* in Mexico was drinking tequila. All across northern Sonora, the name of Emelio Zambrano was feared by brave *hombres*. But I was too slow. His bullet found me."

Luis swallowed hard, silent, remembering.

"Dios spared me . . . He gave me my life. I left Mexico and rode north, to Texas. *Señor* Bill Clay gave me this job. It is better, Tom . . . to sleep at night and work with the cows and horses. I do not think about the past. I am a *vaquero*. It is better."

Tom let a silence pass, remembering a prison cell and the time he'd had to think about his future.

"Wasn't much different for me," he said. "All I want is for folks to leave me alone."

Luis came to his feet and set his sombrero over his eyes.

"There are times when it is hard," he said, like he said it to himself.

At full dark the corrals were repaired and they put their tools away, smelling supper on the woodsmoke from the cabin. Tom trudged to the shed and took the bar of soap and a towel to the pumpjack where he took a bath and put on a set of his new clothing. All afternoon he thought about Luis, liking the man all the more as he worked beside him, the old man's words echoing in Tom's head. It felt good somehow, to find another man who understood the mixture of feelings . . . made him think less about the moment back at the Knickerbocker saloon.

Tom sat on the front porch of the cabin to wait for the evening meal, idly watching Blackie stalk a chicken roosting in a mesquite limb across the yard. The dog crept forward on his belly, pausing when he came close, a silent figure in the darkness that would spell death for the hen unless she stayed watchful. This was a game with Blackie, a game he lost most every time. But it was not a game for the hen and its circumstance reminded Tom of his own. It would pay to keep one eye open and be on the lookout for trouble, and stay clear of a spot where the advantage would belong to the hunter.

When Sara called them to supper she was dressed in a bright calico blouse, cut low in the front, revealing more of her than Tom had ever seen. He felt his appetite draining away, his mind on the creamy skin exposed by her blouse, unable to keep his eyes from straying down to the swell of Sara's breasts.

She smiled at him when they sat around the table. Even Luis took note of the smooth skin of Sara's chest and shoulders.

"You look better, Tom," she said, passing a bowl of ear corn across the table. "It must be the new clothes because your face is still a mess."

He felt his cheeks turn hot when she said it.

"I could wear a bandana over it, I reckon," he said. "Be hard to eat, but I'll do it."

She laughed, showing even white teeth. He wondered what her lips would feel like if he kissed her, deepening the flush in his face when he considered such an outlandish thing.

CHAPTER 8

A WEEK went by, according to the measuring stick Tom used to figure time. No rains came and the river dropped lower, allowing Circle C cattle more shallow places to cross to better pastures west of the Concho. He and Luis spent most of the daylight hours driving cattle back across the river, one eye to the sky in search of rain clouds. On Friday they drove the steer calves away from the corrals and made a sweep up the east bank of the river, looking for strays. In spite of the long hours, Tom was enjoying himself, doing ranch work, allowing his wounds the time to heal.

All week long, both daylight and dark, he thought about Sara Clay while he went about his chores, looking forward to suppertime, awaiting the next moment when he saw her and felt her eyes on him, smiling. He took regular baths, near enough to scrub one layer of skin off his bones it seemed, more baths than he could ever remember. They talked more, over supper, and when she spoke to him his belly fluttered. Even Luis took notice of it, a sly grin touching the corners of his mouth.

Once in a while, when he was off to himself on the ranch aboard the bay, he gave some thought to slipping away from the shed when Luis was asleep to tap on Sara's window . . . maybe ask her to go for a moonlight walk, or sit beside him on the porch. But when he thought about it his knees would turn to jelly and he dismissed it quickly. She would laugh in his face. The looks and smiles she gave him were just her way of being friendly, without the lusty intentions he secretly harbored. He was sure of it, when he reflected on his chances. He had nothing to offer a woman like Sara Clay.

Still, there were times when he thought about it anyway, perhaps to pass some time. He wondered what her body would feel like if he were to hold her tight. She would be soft and warm—he knew it without really knowing.

Saturday, around noon as he was helping Luis mix mortar to repair the stones circling the lip of the well, he straightened up from his work to view a rider in the distance, coming down the wagon road from the east beneath a swirl of dust. Since he'd come to the Clay Ranch there had been no visitors and the sight of the rider touched him with concern.

He wiped off his hands and waited, watching the horseman hurry his sorrel toward the cabin. For a time he could not identify the caller, the distance too great, the rider's face hidden by the shade from his hat brim.

Then he recognized Slim and wondered all the more, until the cowboy rode up to the house and greeted Tom.

"How's things, Tom?" Slim asked, resting an elbow on his saddlehorn.

Tom walked up and shook with Slim, trying to read Slim's face.

"Good enough for a dry year, I reckon," he replied. "If it don't rain we'll blow away around here."

Slim nodded, sweeping a quick look around the ranch. By his face, Tom judged there was something besides a social call on Slim's mind.

"How are things at Triangle Bar?" Tom asked, figuring it was best to get to the heart of matters.

Slim let out a breath.

"We've had a spot of trouble, Tom. Somebody shot the boss down at Comanche Springs. We carried him over to Christoval in the wagon . . . to the doc's office. Doc Spence says it's fifty-fifty he'll make it. Jack lost a lot of blood before we found him."

Tom stiffened when he heard the news.

"It was the railroad men," Tom remarked softly.

Slim agreed with a shake of his head.

"It was the boss who sent me over, Tom. Said he'd like to have a word with you . . . if you could take the time off for the ride to Christoval."

Tom swung a glance toward the house.

"I'll ask Sara . . . Mrs. Clay," he said, turning for the porch.

When he stuck his head through the door he smelled fried chicken, but he was too busy with new worries to think about being hungry.

"What is it, Tom?" Sara asked when he rounded the corner to the kitchen.

"I need a day or two," he replied, watching her face darken, "to ride over to Christoval. Jack Johnson's been shot by some of the railroad bunch. Slim Willis rode over. Jack's been askin' for me, so I reckon I'd better go. Slim says it's pretty bad."

"Of course," she whispered, wiping her hands on her apron. "Take all the time you need."

He wheeled for the door and started out, until her voice stopped him.

"Be careful, Tom," she said. "I wouldn't want anything to happen . . . to you."

He grinned and swung open the door.

"Don't worry. I'll keep my eyes open."

He saddled quickly, his mind tangled with thoughts. Down deep he knew why Johnson had sent for him . . . the Triangle Bar needed his gun more than ever now. As he swung a leg over he made himself a promise, that he'd stay out of the fight 'til hell froze solid. Nothing Jack might say would change his mind.

They rode off under a cloudless sky, pushing their horses, silent for the first few miles. Tom knew there would be talk right at first about the lay of things, then Slim would get around to the purpose for his visit . . . and ask the question Tom dreaded more and more as they headed east.

"It's bad," Slim replied, when Tom asked about Jack's bullet wound. "Right through his shoulder clean, but he damn near bled to death before we found him. He wouldn't let me ride down to the springs with him that day . . . said he'd do it himself."

Tom watched the bay's ears prick forward when a jackrabbit crossed the wagon ruts, thinking about the visit to the doc's office, dreading the moment when he told Jack again that his gun wasn't for hire.

"I talked to the sheriff," Slim said, interrupting Tom's thoughts. "He made a show of bein' real concerned and all, but that's where it'll end. Wired for the Rangers too, like Jack told me. I don't figure it'll be much different than the last time."

"Likely not," Tom agreed.

Slim let a silence pass, watching the land. It would be Slim's way of getting ready to ask Tom for his help, if Tom was any shakes as a guesser.

"Jack put me in charge of things at the ranch," Slim said after a bit. "Wasn't my idea. I've got my hands full, Tom. I don't suppose you'd consider coming back to work for the Triangle bar?"

Tom didn't have to give it another moment's thought.

"I like workin' for Mrs. Clay," he said. "Sorry to hear you're in a fix, but I aim to stay right where I am."

Slim shook his head, like he expected as much. "Figures," he said, letting it drop.

Riding cross-country, they hit the outskirts of Christoval just before dark. False-fronted stores lined a single street in a broad valley. Windows aglow by lanterns shed pale yellow light on the road as they walked their horses to a clapboard building below a sign that read "Dr. Spence," where they got down to tie off their mounts.

Slim knocked on the front door, hitching his thumbs to wait for the door to open. A minute later an elderly gent in shirtsleeves cracked the door and let them in, speaking to Slim as he passed a glance over Tom.

"Come in. He's resting just now. Follow me."

They came down a hallway, to a room off the back. The doctor lit a lantern and walked over to a bed, frowning.

When Tom saw the sleeping face of the rancher he knew things weren't going well. Jack's sun-blackened cheeks were pale and sunken. Beads of sweat covered his forehead, rolling down to the pillow like raindrops.

"You've got a visitor, Jack," Doc Spence said.

Jack opened his eyes, staring first at the ceiling, then toward the men.

"I brought Tom Spoon," Slim said hoarsely.

Jack's eye fell on Tom, flickering.

"Thanks . . . for . . . coming, Tom," he whispered, his voice rasping, hard to hear. "How's Sara?"

"She's fine. Things are okay. It's been dry."

Jack swallowed.

"Need . . . a favor," he said.

Tom made ready for what would come next.

"If I can, Mr. Johnson," he replied, knowing he couldn't.

"My wife . . . if anything happens . . . to me . . ."

Jack's voice trailed off, then he took another breath.

"See she gets . . . on the train . . . to Saint Louis. She has a sister . . ."

This surprised Tom, caught him off guard. All Jack wanted was his wife's safe passage to Saint Louis.

"I can see to it," Tom replied. "I'll see she gets on the train."

Jack's pain-ridden eyes held Tom with a look.

"Don't let Carruthers . . . don't let them force Margaret to sign . . . for the land, Tom. I won't let them beat me."

Tom shook his head, then he had no choice but to look the other way. His conscience shouted at him, cried out to throw in his hand with Jack Johnson just then, begging for the chance to even the odds against the railroad. Right there in the doctor's office he began an argument with himself.

"You can count on it," Tom said evenly. "If anything happens to you, your wife will be on that train."

Jack closed his eyes briefly.

"Give my regards . . . to Sara. It'll rain," he whispered.

"I'll tell her," Tom replied. "Take care of yourself."

Jack's eyes batted open. "Tom, thanks . . . for looking after my wife," he said, then his breathing became regular. "I wish there was more I could do." He was asleep, escaping the pain.

When Slim and Tom walked out of the doctor's office Slim turned to him and said, "I need to make a stop by the sheriff's office, then we'll head back."

They rode down to a tiny storefront affair where a sign decorated one window. Slim swung down to tie off at the rail. For want of a better way to spend the time, Tom joined him.

Inside, Sheriff Baylor and two other men looked up from tin cups of coffee when Slim and Tom came in the office. Tom's glance fell on one of the men, a tall, angular fellow sporting a handlebar mustache with a badge pinned to his leather vest.

The gent studied Tom before he spoke, ignoring Slim for the moment.

"I'll declare," he said without friendliness. "If it ain't Tom Spoon."

The Texas Ranger's eyes went to Tom's waist. Just then Tom wished he had stayed outside on his horse.

"Howdy, Will," Tom said, remembering a time down in San Antonio when neither man had been glad to see the other. Almost twenty years had passed since then.

"I see you've done away with the gun," Will Dobbs said, sounding surprised. Texas Ranger Captain Will Dobbs had been the one handed the chore of advising Tom he'd worn out his welcome in San Antonio . . . after the gunsmoke cleared from the street in front of the Palace Hotel where a Kansas territory shootist named Jack Bibb lay in a pool of blood.

"Got some age on me," Tom replied. "Same as you, Will."

Dobbs put down his cup and came to his feet.

"Seems I heard you did a little time," he said, one hand resting on the butt of his pistol, boring through Tom with a look.

"You've got good ears," Tom said.

"It'd be a shame if you was to take up some of your old ways again," Dobbs said. "You takin' a side in this Concho River business with the railroad?"

"Hadn't yet," Tom answered, glancing at the other men seated around the room. "Just ridin' along."

Dobbs gave a nod, like the idea agreed with him.

"That's good news, Tom. There's been enough gunplay around here. Somebody's tryin' to make it look like the Texas and Pacific is out to get this feller Johnson. We figure it different. All the railroad wants is a line through the property, fair and square. I talked to their agent myself . . . man by the name of Harding Carruthers. Decent sort. He'll pay Johnson's price. Told me so himself."

Slim took a step closer and said his mind.

"Jack Johnson won't sell to the railroad," Slim said. "They can run rails around him."

A stocky gent swung around in his swivel chair, a star on his shirt, facing Slim.

"Johnson's bein' a hard-headed old fool about it," Sheriff Baylor said. "The railroad has offered him a fair price. All this talk about the railroad men shooting Triangle Bar hands is a bunch of nonsense. Looked into it myself. Johnson's tryin' to raise the price on his right-of-way . . . that's what it is."

Slim doubled his fists when he answered.

"The land ain't for sale. Those men were Jack's friends. Snuffy Calhoun worked on the Triangle Bar for twenty years."

The sheriff shook his head and spoke softly. "Some men'll do most anything, for a price. Johnson's behind all this, so he can make himself rich off the railroad."

Slim started toward the sheriff, until Tom touched his arm.

"Take it easy, Slim," he said.

Will Dobbs gave Tom a crooked grin when he saw what Tom had done.

"You're bein' sensible, Tom. We'll look into it, me and my deputy. The Texas and Pacific is an honest outfit. I've had dealings with them before."

Tom went stiff and swung toward Will Dobbs.

"An honest outfit don't need the likes of Odell Pickett," Tom snapped, suddenly angry.

Will blinked, then he twisted one end of his mustache.

"It'd be my advice you stay out of it, Tom," he said.

Tom opened the door, then he hesitated and gave the sheriff a glare.

"You can figure on one thing," Tom said, speaking in a low voice. "Jack Johnson is a friend of mine."

He walked out to the boardwalk boiling mad . . . at himself for opening his mouth to Will Dobbs, and at the lawmen who were taking the railroad's side in the issue. He took a deep breath before he stepped in a stirrup, deciding he would put the whole mess behind him and stay wide of it. The only promise he'd give was to be certain Margaret Johnson made it to the train if Jack lost his fight with a bullet wound.

When they swung south down the street he decided another thing . . . he was too close to his home range to escape his past. When spring rolled around he would pack his gear and ride west, to the New Mexico territory like he had intended. It was better, to be clear of an old reputation he wanted to forget. Some folks just wouldn't let it lie. Everywhere he turned, he found a reminder.

Slim rode up beside him, silent until they were out of town under a starry sky.

"Thanks for coming, Tom," Slim said. "And thanks for what you said back at the sheriff's office. Seems a lot of folks know you from before. It may not help much, but if they think you're siding with us they might leave us alone."

"You're up against long odds, Slim," he said. "Those lawmen are taking the railroad's side. And there's Pickett. I don't figure you stand much of a chance against so many."

"I see it the same way," Slim answered. "I ain't got much choice. I owe the bossman . . . Jack gave me a job when there wasn't any to be had. If I ran out on him now, I couldn't live with it long. I aim to stay. It don't matter about the odds."

Tom thought about it, forced to admire Slim for his stand. Old feelings awakened inside him, the ones that once made him too hot-headed to pass up a fight. And his bad temper had already landed him in prison once. He kept that last thought in mind as they rode back to the Triangle Bar fence.

"Good luck with it, Slim," he said, halting his horse beside the wire gap where Slim dismounted. "I'll hand you some free advice. There's some men who make a profession out of a gun. That's what you're up against. A smart feller knows when he's licked."

Slim opened the gate and led his horse through.

"Could be, Tom. Times, there's other things to think about too . . . like what you owe a man who is a friend. Most don't get but one or two good friends in a lifetime."

Slim swung in his saddle and gathered his reins.

"Be seein' you, Tom," he said before he spurred his horse away from the fence.

At sunup he rode down to the Circle C on a lathered horse, just as Luis left the shed for the house.

"How is *Señor* Johnson?" Luis asked when Tom was out of the saddle.

"He looks near 'bout dead to me," Tom replied, pulling his cinch. "I don't figure his chances very high."

"The railroad?" Luis said, a question.

"Likely. Nothing else makes any sense."

Luis waited until Tom's saddle was hung, then they walked together toward the house, smelling breakfast.

"They want you to help with your gun," Luis said, to say he understood the visit from Slim Willis.

"That's about the size of it. I won't do it, Luis. I swore I'd never tie on a gun again. Much as I'd like to help out, I damn sure won't do it with a pistol."

Luis shook his head, agreeing silently.

Luis went inside while Tom went to the pump to wash the trail dust from his face and hands. While he worked the pump handle he passed a milestone of sorts. Blackie came over to him, wagging his tail, allowing Tom to pat him on top of his head. It was the first sign the dog had given that he was glad to see Tom, a sign that things were changing at the Circle C for Tom Spoon.

The table was spread with platters of eggs and bacon and golden biscuits. Jars of jelly sat beside the coffee pot. When Tom took his usual chair, Sara came over to put her arm around his neck, then she took him by surprise and bent over to plant a kiss against his cheek.

"We missed you," she said, chuckling. "How was Jack Johnson?"

Tom was too flustered to think clearly for a time, until he saw Sara take her chair across the table. Her kiss was almost too much good luck for him to take in one swallow, tangling the words he wanted to say before he could get them lined up on his tongue.

"It's pretty bad," he said when he could think straight, noting the grin on Luis' face. "The doctor says it's even odds that he'll live."

"Poor Jack," Sara sighed, staring absently at her plate. "It's that damn railroad business."

It was the first cussword he'd heard from her since he came to the ranch, understandable under the circumstances. He quickly forgot the brief kiss and put his mind on the conversation.

"Jack extracted a promise from me. If anything happens to him, I'm to see to it that his wife gets on the train to Saint Louis before the railroad agents try to make her sign over the right-of-way."

Sara nodded thoughtfully. "He won't give in, no matter what," she said. "That would be just like him."

Tom took a helping of eggs and bacon, thinking back to his visit to the doctor's office and the sheriff.

"He's in a fight he can't win," Tom said. "The local sheriff and the Texas Rangers have set their sights on him . . . taken the railroad's side. It's a sure bet the folks in town want that

rail line close, instead of south fifty miles around the Triangle
Bar. That pretty well stacks most everybody against Jack."

Sara looked up quickly. "He's within his legal rights, Tom.
It's his land."

Tom shrugged and dug into his breakfast. "Maybe so, Sara,
but he can't win against the odds."

Sara's eyes flashed angrily. "If the same thing was happening to me, I'd fight them all."

Tom watched her, thinking she probably would.

"Even if you'd had three good men killed, and another
shot and maybe dyin'?" he asked.

She hesitated, still angry, thinking. Then she let her shoulders sag and stirred her eggs.

"No. I couldn't sit by and let them kill either one of you,"
she said, softer now. "Why can't the law do something?"

"It's my guess the Christoval Sheriff is on the railroad's
payroll," he replied. "Maybe they've promised him a bigger
town and higher wages when the rails come through. Then
there's a Ranger Captain I met . . . knew him before. A blind
man can see he's hooked up with the Texas and Pacific
somehow. Likely a payoff to turn the other way if they have
any trouble. With so many siding against the Triangle Bar, it
don't stand much of a chance."

Sara stared at him across the table.

"Jack wants you to help him, doesn't he?" she asked. "He
needs a man who can use a gun."

Tom sighed, looking the other way.

"That's about the size of it," he said.

"Don't do it, Tom," she said. "You've got a job here, for as
long as I can stay in the cattle business. We'll make it, if it'll
rain."

"I don't aim to, Sara. I don't carry a gun any more."

She gave him a smile, the kind that made his belly flop.

"It isn't your affair," she said.

"*Verdad,*" Luis remarked, to say it was the truth.

Following breakfast Tom went out on the porch, deciding he would spend Sunday breaking a paint colt in one of the corrals to a saddle. With so many cattle scattering west of the river he needed another ranch horse, to lighten the work on his bay.

He was sleepy after the all-night ride, choosing a short nap first before he took on the spotted colt. Blackie followed him to the shed, wagging his tail, making Tom feel more at home than ever. He wondered if he could do it . . . ride off when spring came to New Mexico territory. He was starting to like it here, and there was the woman, the way she made him feel when he was close to her. Could be he'd stay, after he thought about it.

The bronc two-year-old shivered when Tom ran a hand down his neck, humping his back under the empty saddle, ready to explode. He had fought the rope, then the feel of the cinch, rearing and pawing at the two-legged creature who worked around him.

"Easy there, son," Tom said, grinning at the colt's effort to fight the strange restraints. "I ain't gonna hurt you. Take it easy."

Tom felt Sara's eyes on him, watching from the shade of the porch. Luis stood outside the corral, leaned over a rail. Tom ran his hands over the frightened gelding, talking softly, waiting for the sound of his voice and the gentle feel of his hands to calm the paint some. Tied to a fence post, the horse could do little besides take what the man did to him, snorting, legs trembling with fear over a first saddling.

Tom pulled the slip knot in the rope and stuck one boot in a stirrup. Before the colt knew what Tom was about, he was over the saddle, getting set for the ride.

Suddenly the paint downed his head and tried to buck the

weight off his back, crow-hopping away from the fence, bawling with fright. Tom grinned when he felt the green attempt to spill a rider. The paint didn't know how to buck, hadn't learned the finer art of dirty moves to unseat a cowboy. If Tom had his way with the horse, he wouldn't let him learn.

Tom pulled the rope and drove his spurs into the gelding's ribs. The colt jumped, surprised by the stab of the rowels, then he broke into a run around the corral fence, trying to escape the punishment of a spur. Tom let him run, let him have his head to tire himself out in the gallop around the fence.

Every now and then the paint slowed and tried to pitch again, and each time Tom stuck his spurs into the spotted hide to spook the horse back into a run. The colt would learn, given the time, that the spurs came only when he tried to buck. Later, he would learn more about a spur, and the touch of a rein across his neck. For now, it was enough to learn that pitching would earn him the sharp pain of a rowel.

Flanks heaving, the paint finally slowed and trotted to a halt after a half hour of circles around the pen. Tom pulled back on the colt's nose and ran a hand down his neck, talking softly all the while, reassuring the horse that he had done what the man expected of him.

"Easy, boy. Smart critter, ain't you?" Tom said.

When the gelding was calmed to the feel of a rider on his back Tom eased his right foot out of the stirrup and dismounted slowly. The colt snorted when he saw the man on the ground beside him, unable to figure the change. Tom rubbed the paint's nose, allowing him the chance to get Tom's man-smell. The colt would recognize the smell when Tom saddled him again, making the job a little easier.

"You are good with a *caballo*," Luis offered when Tom led the colt to the gate.

"Thanks," Tom said with a shrug. "A green colt don't test a man too much if he'll take the time. I needed a spare, as much ground as we've had to cover lately. If it don't rain pretty soon, I'm liable to need another."

Tom led the paint toward the shed, past the porch where Sara sat watching him. He glanced her way and found her smiling, putting the flutter into his chest, again.

"Nice job of it," she said. "You've got a gentle way with horses, Tom."

"Plenty of practice," he said, pausing briefly. "About all I've done with my life is ride a horse and swing a rope and . . ."

He didn't finish, didn't make mention of using a gun. He led the colt toward the shed and stripped off the saddle, trying for all he was worth to keep his mind from the sight of Jack Johnson at the doctor's office, the feeling of guilt he carried on his shoulders for not offering the Triangle Bar a hand with the railroad agents while Jack lay on the edge of death. The argument went on in spite of his efforts to silence his conscience, the nagging voice that said he could put an end to Jack's troubles with Odell Pickett and his gunmen.

He had no doubts about taking Pickett with a gun . . . he'd done it once before . . . had the chance to kill him; instead he had aimed for an arm. The others, the mean-eyed boy who kicked him across the saloon, the other young toughs who rode with Pickett, would be too slow, too anxious for good aim, making the mistakes that killed most of their kind sooner or later when they drew against a man with experience.

It would all be so easy, until the smoke cleared away and the lawmen came to arrest the survivor, and then there'd be the rest of Tom's years locked in a cage. He simply could not do it. His only option would be to run for the Mexican border and hide from the law until he died of old age.

Thus he put his plan aside, knowing it was temporary, until the little voice woke up again inside his head. Then the argument would start all over again and he would be wrestling with the idea once more, grinding his teeth with frustration, wishing things could be different somehow.

He took his rope and walked down to the corrals to catch the bay. In the shade of the saddle shed he took a rasp and a new set of horseshoes and went about the business of paring off the bay's hooves for new iron, working up a powerful sweat in the late afternoon heat, keeping his mind off other matters. Luis sat in the shade whittling on a green stick with his pocket knife, covering his boots with slender shavings while Tom went about the shoeing.

Blackie stalked a chicken to one side of the shed, creeping on his belly, following the hen as it pecked around the yard. A stiff breeze turned the blades atop the windmill tower, rattling the pump shaft that lifted precious water in irregular spurts into a big stone trough.

Tom heard the sounds and kept one eye on Blackie while he finished the shoeing job, deciding he had grown comfortable with the sights and sounds of the ranch, feeling more at home all the time. Most of his life had been spent on the move, never staying in one place long enough to call it home, constantly drifting from one job to the next. It felt good, the way things were now, like he belonged to a place, adding fuel to the argument that it would be a mistake to risk it all by strapping on his gun to meddle in someone else's affairs.

He was done before dark, turning the bay into the corral with the paint colt.

"I'll ride you again tomorrow," he said, watching the spotted horse back away from him warily. "By the end of the week you'll be pushing longhorns across the river . . . maybe have one tied to you by a rope. You're set to find out what it's like to work for a living."

He rested his elbows on the fence and swung a look around the shallow valley . . . the scattered live oaks and mesquites and dry bunchgrass across the hills. He felt at peace with himself, relaxed and enjoying life. Making a living with a gun had never permitted such a calm, not allowed him the time to grow accustomed to surroundings, or the time to make a friend. A shootist could not afford a friend or any attachments to people and places. There was always the chance that a friend would betray you, sell you out for a better payday, gun you down from the back side. And there was the constant need to keep on the move, from job to job, always on the alert for a backshooter.

It hadn't seemed so bad before, when he was younger. The pay was good. Age, and a prison stretch, had changed the way he felt about it. There was no reason that was good enough to go back to his old life with a gun.

When he turned away from the fence he found Sara behind him, watching him. He couldn't guess how long she'd been standing there without his notice.

"Must have been some deep thinking going on," she said.

"Plenty," he sighed, grinning, wondering what else to say. "Had a lot to think about, lately."

She came toward him, smelling of soap, blond curls framing the soft lines of her face. Her eyes smiled, wrinkling the way they always did around the corners, making him feel weak in the knees. She wore tight denims and the low-cut blouse, revealing more of herself than he wished she had just then. A red sunset turned her skin to copper, smooth as cream. He felt things stirring in his groin, certain that his cheeks were turning pink.

"You are . . . a beautiful woman, Sara," he said, wondering why his voice was so different, like he had gravel in his throat.

"Why, thank you, Tom," she said, smiling. "I didn't know you noticed a woman. It's nice of you to say it."

"It wasn't proper . . . just thought I'd make the observation," he mumbled, feeling like his tongue was tied in a knot.

"It was very proper, Tom."

The smile faded on her face and she took a step closer, her eyes locked on his, bigger than he remembered them. His mind filled with a thousand thoughts at once while he fished around for the right thing to say.

"It'll be a nice evening, after it cools," he said, feeling his heart hammer inside his shirt. "Might be a good time to take a walk around the place."

She tilted her head, like maybe she hadn't heard him quite right the first time.

"I'd like that," she whispered, "later, after it cools off."

She was gone before he could think, before he could nod his head or say yes to the idea, walking toward the cabin. His glance fell on her hips, the sway, and the roundness.

"Damn it all, Spoon," he muttered. "Now you've gone and done it . . . got your foot stuck in a bucket."

At supper he felt like a tomcat under a rocking chair, too nervous to eat, minding his manners, smelling the rose hair tonic he'd splashed over his grey mane. If Sara noticed she gave no sign, making small talk with Luis over the pastures and the dry river. Tom hardly ate a bite of his stew, found the cornbread too dry and almost choked on it. When their meal was over he was thankful and glad to have the opportunity to step out on the porch with Luis while Sara cleared the table.

A skyful of stars blinked down from an inky black sky. Tom found it hard to make conversation, worrying about the anticipated walk with Sara. He couldn't count the years since he'd been with a woman, many more since it was a proper woman. Most of his time had been spent with saloon whores, hardly the place to learn conduct with a lady. Right up 'til now it hadn't mattered much. Tonight it would show through like a hole in his hat.

He made a try at conversation with Luis, then failure at it made him walk off to the shed, pretending sleep was his purpose. He lay down on his bunk and closed his eyes, shivering like a newborn calf on a cold morning.

He tiptoed away from the shed when Luis snored, then he straightened himself when he thought about what he might look like crossing to the house, bent over like a thief with a sack full of chickens. He walked slowly to the front, searching the darkness below the porch, and caught his breath when he saw Sara seated in a chair.

"Nice night, isn't it?" she asked.

"Real nice night," he said, making a show of looking casually at the sky. "Nice night for a walk," he said, thinking how rehearsed he sounded.

"I'll join you, if you don't mind," she replied, coming to her feet. "Let's walk up on the hill so we can see the valley."

She came to him, smelling sweet, like flowers. She took his hand gently in her own and gave him one of her smiles. He did not grip her hand too tightly, even though it was an effort. He gazed down at her soft hair and smiling face, dizzy with the smell of her and the way she looked in the light from the full moon.

He started to walk away from the house, until the pressure of her hand stopped him in midstride. She lifted one hand and placed her palm against his cheek, moving close to his chest, opening her mouth so he could see the dark lines of her parted lips across her white teeth.

"Kiss me, Tom," she said, a whisper of breath from her mouth, lifting on her toes to reach him.

"I'm not much good at it, Sara," he said hoarsely.

She moved her fingers to the back of his neck, tangling them in his curls, pulling his face down. Her lips came over his mouth, as warm and soft as he imagined they would be. Her arm tightened around his neck and she let go of his hand to wrap the other arm around him.

He felt her body against him, and lifted his hands to her tiny waist, careful not to squeeze too tightly, afraid he might break her in half.

A soft moan came from deep inside her chest. The swell of her breasts touched him, pressing against his shirt. His skin began to tingle as he felt her fingers dig into his neck. She made little sounds in her throat, tightening her embrace, moving against him.

His mouth was wet from her kiss when she pulled away.

"Let's go inside, Tom," she whispered.

She took him by the hand and led him toward the cabin, then into the bedroom to a big four-poster bed.

CHAPTER 9

JUST before the first grey streaks of dawn came to the sky he crept into the shed and lay across his bunk. Luis snored softly. Tom's entrance went unnoticed.

He was filled with pleasant memories of Sara's soft skin and tender embraces. When they came together on the mattress they made love until they both were spent, his desire no less than her own. Later, there were whispered words while they held each other, sharing the loneliness of their lives. He had never known another woman like her . . . she made him feel comfortable, able to say things he'd never said to a woman before. Touching her, holding her close to his chest, sent an odd sensation through him. Being with Sara gave him feelings that were new to him, strange and wonderful.

Love was a word he never understood. He'd never felt anything he could have called love, mostly a simple physical need when it came to women. But tonight's short hours had taught him many new things, how two people could be drawn to each other to find parts of themselves they didn't know before. It surprised him, that he had a gentler side, capable of tender loving and deep feelings for another. It was brand new, like the first few days wearing a store-bought beaver fur hat, the first moments unfamiliar, aware of the newness, until it started to fit around his head.

Sara was like that . . . scaring him at first, until he allowed himself the openness bottled up inside that came much more easily for her, it seemed. She whispered things in his ear, and to his great surprise he said the same things and felt the same way. His need matched hers, slower to come out in the beginning, as self-conscious as he was. Making love to Sara was so very different from his experiences with other women . . . impossible to compare.

"Now, what do I do?" he asked himself quietly while Luis slept. "I'm stuck like an overloaded wagon in a muddy ditch. I can't just ride off in the spring. Sara has branded me like one of her calves. She'll own me."

He did not find the thought unpleasant. Troubling, when he gave it more thought, but hardly a thing to worry him. Being tied to Sara Clay wasn't such a bad idea, when he gave it a closer look.

When he and Luis walked in for breakfast, Tom found himself in an awkward moment, one he hadn't prepared for. When he saw Sara he felt a hot flush creep up his face, reminded of their intimate hours in her bedroom. With Luis at the dining room table, Tom was suddenly self-conscious. He vowed to act as naturally as he could in spite of the change in his coloration and the shaky feeling in his fingers. He was unaccountably embarrassed just then, and it puzzled him.

Sara greeted them in the same fashion she did most every morning, with her smile.

"Good morning, Tom. Good morning, Luis," she said.

It might have been his imagination, but he would have bet a new hat that there was a difference in the way she looked at him, her eyes lingering on his face a bit longer than before.

"Mornin', Sara," he mumbled, hoping there was no change in his voice or his manner that Luis would notice.

He sat while Sara poured coffee. When she came to the

table she smiled at him again. In spite of himself he squirmed in his chair.

"Wish it would rain," he said, a feeble attempt to put everyone's attention on something else.

"Maybe it will," she said, still watching his face, still smiling.

"I'll ride east this morning," he said, wishing she would look the other way so he could collect his thoughts. "I'll check the windmill and the east fence."

"I will ride the river," Luis said, forking hotcakes onto his plate, then ladling them with generous spoonfuls of honey. "The water grows lower every day."

Sara sat across the table from Tom. He felt her eyes on him as he prepared his hotcakes. He forced his attention to his plate and tried to eat slowly.

"We'll have to buy feed for the winter," Sara said, "or sell off part of the herd before fall. The grass won't hold out unless it rains pretty soon."

"Not a cloud in the sky all week," Tom said, discovering that he had no appetite.

They finished their meal in silence. When Luis' plate was empty he tossed in his fork and shoved back his chair.

"It will be a long day," he said, climbing to his feet. "On the way to the river I will ask *Dios* for the rain."

Tom meant to walk out behind Luis, to escape the uncomfortable feeling of being alone with Sara. He started out of his chair with every intention of hurrying for the door.

"Tom," she said, halting him in his tracks, "what's wrong? You hardly looked at me this morning."

He hitched his thumbs in his pockets, to keep his hands from shaking.

"I ain't exactly sure," he said, taking his eyes from the floor where he'd purposefully kept them. "I can't come up with any answer that makes sense," he shrugged, feeling his cheeks turn hot again.

"Was it . . . last night?," she asked softly.

He saw a look on her face he'd never seen before, like something he'd said or done had hurt her.

"No . . . that ain't it at all. Last night was nigh onto perfect, Sara. Maybe that's it? . . . could be it was too perfect. I never met a woman like you before. I guess I'm not rightly sure how to act just now."

"You shouldn't feel that way," she whispered. "It happened, and I don't want it to change things . . . between us."

Tom scuffed a boot toe against the floor.

"I've been a loner all my life," he said, hoping that his speech-making would come out right. "Never was taught how to act around a woman. I said a bucketful of words last night an' that ain't my natural way. This mornin', I'm plumb out of words."

Sara folded her hands into her apron.

"I've been alone a long time, too," she said, looking around the cabin briefly. "I made up my mind after my husband died that I'd have to make do on this ranch by myself, just me and Luis. I never wanted another man . . . until I met you. I can't explain it properly."

Self-conscious again, he fumbled for the right answer.

"I ain't much to look at, Sara, and I've only got a few dollars to my name. I reckon it surprised me, when you . . ."

He couldn't say it. The words got stuck in his mouth.

"None of that matters to me, Tom, not the money. I liked you the first time I saw you. Last night was special. Don't let it change things for us."

She came around the table, then she stood on tiptoes to kiss him.

"Good luck with the windmill," she said, turning for the kitchen before he had the time to think of his answer.

He rode cross-country, on the lookout for wandering cattle grazing the sparse grass. The wild longhorns had a tendency to stay in small groups in dry weather, the cows bunched with a particular bull as they ranged farther to find food. It made for a tougher roundup, having to gather so many herds in open country.

Just before noon he topped a rise and saw trouble ahead, around the windmill. Better than a hundred head of long-horns milled about near the watering trough, too many to be Circle C cattle. The fence would be down again, and likely cut by the railroad men.

He spurred the bay to a lope and rode up to the windmill, discovering Triangle Bar brands on most of the loose-hided cows. Then he took note of the water level in the stone trough, pulled down by so many thirsty cattle. A dry wind whistled through the windmill's blades, working the sucker rod rapidly. But no water came from the length of pipe, the rod rattling dryly above the sounds of bawling cattle.

He tied off the bay and braked the windmill, its shaft screaming in protest when the brake fought the stiff wind. He carried a tin cup of water from the trough and tried to prime the pump, failing the first time, then the second, and the third.

The well's gone dry, he thought. The water level has dropped without rain.

When he swung a look around he found loose wires hanging limply from fence posts as far as he could see both north and south.

"They did a job on it this time," he said to himself. "It's cut in more than one spot, if I'm any judge."

He cussed under his breath and gave up on priming the pump, swinging into the saddle for a ride up the fence. He didn't have far to ride before he found busted wires. When he made a splice and tried to tighten a wire, it pulled too easily in his gloved hands. The fence was cut some place farther north, out of sight over a hilltop.

He made the mends and left them limp, riding north to a second cut where he performed the same chore and felt the same result when he tried the strands. North again, he found two more holes in the fence over a two-mile stretch. Someone wanted to make sure the wires stayed down this time.

The hoofprints of two horses led away from every cut in the barbed wire. Tom followed them with his eyes, north again over a rise. These tracks were fresh . . . sharp-edged, maybe only a few hours old. Tom studied the prints, gazing north.

"Damn it all," he muttered, swinging up from his last repair to follow the tracks. "It'll take me and Luis a full day to sort through those cows."

He rode over a grassy knoll and checked rein. A riderless horse wandered along a ridge in the distance, trailing its reins, grazing. The empty saddle was a sign of big trouble. A man on foot, maybe bucked off the back of a bronc, lying hurt some place, or worse.

Tom spurred to a lope, riding the fence with a careful eye. When he came to a dry wash down in a swale he saw a sight that made him spur the bay harder . . . a man lay at the bottom of the wash, sprawled on his back, motionless.

He recognized the boy before he jumped down from his saddle, the kid from the Triangle Bar called Lucky, the one who'd been pitched off his horse before dawn. A second look was proof the boy hadn't been thrown this time . . . a dark bloodstain covered the front of his shirt, spread over the caliche ground.

Tom ran to the spot and knelt down, examining the hole in Lucky's chest. Blood seeped from the wound, drying in the heat of the sun where it flowed down his shirt.

"Can you hear me, kid?" he asked, peeling back the lid of one closed eye.

Lucky's eyes batted open, staring blankly at the sky.

"Hurts . . ." the boy croaked, twisting his mouth when he said it. "Bad . . ."

Tom tore off a piece of the boy's sleeve and stuffed it in the bullet hole, bringing more pain to Lucky's face.

"Hold on, son. I'll catch your horse and get you to a doctor."

Lucky lifted a hand and closed it around Tom's arm.

"Don't leave me," he said weakly. "Please . . . stay."

Tom clamped his jaw. It was easy to see the boy was dying, the color drained from his face, a haze clouding his eyes.

"I'll be right here. Did you see who shot you?"

He gave a weak nod, then his lips quivered when he spoke.

"Pickett," he stammered, stiffening when fresh pain went through him. "One more . . . two guns."

The boy's left foot twitched beyond his control. Glassy eyes fell on Tom, bulging from their sockets. Lucky tried to speak, wanted to say more. A gust of wind swept dust into his open mouth, over the glazed eyes. Tom reached down and took the kid's hand, squeezing it.

"It won't hurt much longer, son," he said.

Ragged breath came from Lucky's mouth, gurgling wetly. The bullet had gone through a lung. Foamy blood spilled from the corners of the boy's lips, trickling down his cheeks to the ground.

Tom looked away, tightening his grip on Lucky's hand. He knew the boy would not last much longer. As hard as it was to stay and watch it, he knew he couldn't leave until it was over.

Minutes later, Lucky took a deep breath and went still. Tom knelt beside him several minutes more, then he pried the boy's frozen fingers from his arm and placed his hand across his chest.

Tom stood up slowly and dusted off his knees. He tilted his head toward the sky and wondered out loud . . . "Why the kid? He was hardly old enough to shave."

On wooden legs, Tom went to his bay and mounted, then he rode back to catch Lucky's horse and led it to the swale where he lifted the body, tying it across the saddle with his lariat.

At a walk, he started toward the Triangle Bar, leading the horse bearing the kid's body. He tried to push it from his mind, but without result. Gusts of wind swept dust around the horses, a reminder of short rainfall. But Tom's thoughts were elsewhere . . . on the boy. Rain wouldn't wash the blood from his memory, or the last moments of Lucky's life with his fingers clutching Tom's arm when he died.

It was full dark, around midnight, when Tom rode down to the corrals where he had ridden the grey stallion, earning the fifty dollars he needed so desperately. Fate had drawn him to the Triangle Bar that day like a rope tied to a maverick calf. He'd been on his way to New Mexico territory, perhaps even on to California, to start a new life away from his past. He'd almost made it, too, earning the money, fixed to make the ride with a grubstake in his pockets. If only he had ridden on, like he intended. Lady Luck made her play instead, teasing him into staying with a job . . . and the woman.

"Damn the luck," he mumbled, leading the horse to the front of the bunk house. "Spoon luck, that's what it is."

The sounds of the horseshoes brought men out in the dark, rifles hung loosely in nervous hands. Slim came first, one eye on the body draped over the saddle, the other on Tom.

"It's Lucky," he said. "Some of the men are out looking for him because he didn't come back for supper."

Tom handed Slim the reins on Lucky's horse and shook his head.

"I found him along the fence," Tom said. "Before he died he told me it was Pickett who shot him. Saddle a horse and we'll ride over to Christoval and tell the sheriff . . . and Will Dobbs, if he's still around. This oughta be enough to have Pickett and his men arrested for murder. I'll tell 'em what the boy told me."

Slim started for the barn at a trot, then he stopped and swung around to face Tom.

"They won't believe you, Tom. They'll say it's your word against Pickett's."

"Let's give it a try," Tom replied softly.

They tied off at the hitchrail with the sun three hours high, climbing to the boardwalk in front of the Sheriff's office. Tom went in first, finding the barrel-chested sheriff in his chair muddling over a stack of papers on his desk, a look of surprise on his face when he saw Tom and Slim enter the office.

"What's for you gents, today?," he asked, wary, handing them a look of caution.

"A man's been killed at the Triangle Bar," Tom said. "A kid by the name of Lucky Stiles. I found him yesterday. Before he died he told me it was Odell Pickett and one of Pickett's men who shot him. Slim, here, is foreman at the ranch. He's here to swear out a warrant for Pickett's arrest on a murder charge."

"Hold on a minute there, Spoon," the sheriff said. "First off, I ain't sure I'll take the word of a convicted killer on such a serious charge. Odell Pickett is a legal deputy of the Texas and Pacific railroad. Captain Dobbs told me about you.

I'd have to make an investigation of the charges . . . before I'd believe the word of an outlaw. Unless you've got a witness, it's your word against that of Mr. Pickett. I'll look into it."

Tom went stiff and balled his hands.

"I was there," Tom snapped. "I'm your witness."

The sheriff shook his head.

"Ain't enough, Spoon. We don't cotton to killers around here. Christoval is a quiet place . . . honest folks. We hold to law and order in this town. Mr. Pickett is a lawman, too, same as me. I ain't gonna ride out to that railroad camp and make a charge against Mr. Pickett . . . not without some proof. I told you I'd look into it."

Slim took a step toward the desk.

"Listen to me, Sheriff Baylor," he said, holding his temper the best he could. "You know what's going on. They've killed four of our hands . . . and wounded Jack to boot. Our fences have been cut and our cattle scattered all over creation. You've gone too far this time, Joe Don. Bein' sheriff don't make you any different than the rest of us. Take a walk outside this office and I'll show you a thing or two . . . bare fisted, if you're man enough to unbuckle that gun."

Joe Don Baylor came to his feet, glowering first at Slim, then at Tom.

"I'm gonna give you some advice, Willis. Unless you want to spend some time in my jail, you'd better get on your horse and ride out of Christoval. Hangin' around with the likes of Tom Spoon makes matters worse. There ain't a jury in this county who'd believe a word Tom Spoon had to say. Get out of my office. Get out of my town, before I run you out, or lock you up in jail."

Slim backed off and turned for the door.

"You've been bought and paid for, Joe Don," he said, then he jerked open the door and stormed out on the boardwalk.

blame 'em much. Be careful yourself, Tom. You could get caught in the crossfire."

Slim rode away, talking to himself. Tom waited until he was out of sight, then he looked west toward the Circle C, only a glance before he reined the bay east toward the railroad camp, the sun at his back.

CHAPTER 10

HE rode off a bluff above the rail camp in the fading light of late evening, holding the bay in an easy dogtrot, cussing his bad luck to be born with an inclination to meddle in affairs that weren't his. He'd stood by about as long as he could . . . had run away from it, if the truth was told. Some men were made differently. Some could turn the other way when a wrong came about, keep their noses out of someone else's business 'til hell froze over. Spoon blood flowed the other way, in his experience. He wasn't the type who could walk off with his hands in his pockets and leave it alone. He had to try something.

He rode past the scattered tents, toward the rail cars with a set to his mouth, wondering how things would go. A man like Odell Pickett wouldn't scare easy, backed by four or five gunhands with the authority of a railroad badge pinned to his chest. It was a gamble, to make a try at talking Pickett out of more killing. There was only a slim chance Pickett would back off.

When he rode up to the last rail car he spotted three men squatting around a campfire near a group of hobbled horses, their eyes on him as he reined down on the bay. Their gunbelts told him all he needed to know . . . they were Pickett's men.

One of the three stood up, fisting a bottle of whiskey when he came toward Tom, his right hand dangling near the butt of his pistol.

"You got business here?" he asked, sullen about it, a hard look across his face.

"Tell Pickett that Tom Spoon is here to see him," Tom said, placing both hands on his saddlehorn, in plain sight.

The gunman gave Tom a careful look.

"I'll tell him," he said, then he climbed slowly into the back of the car.

Tom sat, one eye on the windows, awaiting the arrival of Pickett, still mad at himself for the choice he'd made. Without a gun there would be nothing more than talk. For now. When the talking ended the trouble would start, if Tom was any judge.

The door opened. First to come out was the boy, the one who made a fool of Tom at Knickerbocker. Then Pickett came to take a stand beside him on the narrow platform across the back of the car, fixing his eyes on Tom.

"Surprised to see you, Tom," he said, speaking in the same hoarse voice Tom remembered. "Surprised you still ain't carryin' a gun."

Pickett wore a black broadcloth suit, pants stuffed into tall boots, a black vest, and a white shirt. His flat brim covered his eyes, pulled low in the front. He wore a badge . . . and a gunbelt tied low against his right leg. Ropelike arms hung at his sides.

"Came for some plain talk, Odell," Tom said, watching the boy at Pickett's side, the pair of pistols in cutaway holsters. "This business with Johnson has gone far enough. I didn't aim to take a side in it, so long as things stayed square. When you shot that kid yesterday, you took a step over my fences. The boy didn't carry a gun."

"Who said I shot him?" Pickett asked, wearing the beginnings of a one-sided grin.

"The boy," Tom replied evenly. "I rode up on him, just before he died."

Pickett laughed.

"He had a rifle, Spoon. Me an' Monty rode that fence, mindin' our own business, headed for a little place called Knickerbocker. The cowboy went for his rifle. Didn't leave me and Monty no choice."

"I say you're a liar, Odell," Tom snapped. "You gunned down that boy."

Pickett's right hand went stiff.

"You're buyin' yourself a pine box, Spoon. Nobody calls me a liar."

Tom tightened his grip on his saddlehorn.

"I just did," Tom replied, "and I came to give you fair warning. Next fence that goes down on the Johnson spread . . . next shot that gets fired, I'm comin' for you, Odell. You'll be bettin' your life on it, if you ignore my warning."

A silence passed between them, their eyes locked in a deadly stare. Then Pickett got an amused look on his face.

"Monty tells me you ain't got much left, Tom," he said, chuckling. "Said you went out of that saloon on your hands and knees. Things are different now. You're an old man, Tom. I can take you. You're too damn old and too damn slow."

Monty sidled to the edge of the platform.

"I can take you on the best day you ever had, Tom Spoon," he said. "Go get your gun, old-timer. You don't scare me."

Tom lifted his reins and made ready to ride.

"Remember what I said. Next time there won't be any time wasted with talk."

Tom wheeled the bay and trotted away from the car, teeth clamped hard to keep more words inside his mouth. Like he guessed, the ride over had been a waste of time, but he'd done it. His conscience would be clear. They had his warning.

Bent into the wind, Tom rode past the campfires to high

ground. When the rail camp was behind him he allowed the
bay to slow to a walk. Too long without sleep, he rested in the
saddle and tried to put his mind on other things. When his
anger subsided he thought back to the night spent with Sara,
remembering her soft skin and the whispered words they
shared, good feelings of a kind he hadn't known before, with
a promise of more in the weeks and months to come.

He was risking it all, taking a stand against Odell Pickett
and the railroad. If it came down to gunplay, he would have
no choice but to ride away from it when it was finished. Will
Dobbs and Joe Don Baylor would see to it that Tom Spoon
was not welcome in these parts . . . maybe even have him
thrown in a jail cell. Again. A hot temper would cost him his
freedom. It was one hell of a gamble to take.

Past midnight, closer to dawn, he rode down to the ranch
half-asleep in his saddle, listening to Blackie bark at him
until the dog recognized him in the darkness. He put the
gelding away and walked tiredly to the shed, falling across
his bunk without taking off his clothes. One last thought
crossed his mind before his eyes closed . . . what it would be
like to feel the weight of a gun around his waist after so
many years . . . what it would be like to send a hand toward
the butt of his pistol with the intentions of killing the man
who filled his sights.

He awoke at first light and rolled over on his back. A shaft
of sunlight fell across his face from the window, reminding
him that today was a workday just like any other. Luis was at
the mirror shaving off his whiskers, glancing over at Tom
when Tom swung a leg off his bunk.

"You talk in your sleep, *compadre*," Luis said. "A dream."

"Sorry," Tom mumbled, rubbing his eyes. "Had a lot on
my mind lately."

"The bosslady worried when you did not come for supper.

She sent me over to the well. I found your tracks . . . and the blood on the ground."

Tom nodded sleepily.

"The railroad agents killed another one of the Triangle Bar riders. I found him. Wasn't much choice but to carry him over to the Johnson place. I'll explain to Sara at breakfast."

Luis grinned through a faceful of shaving soap.

"The lady has her eye on you, Tom," he said.

"I know," he replied. "I feel the same for her, Luis. I never met another woman like her."

Luis nodded, shaving his chin.

"It is good. To have a woman."

"Maybe. Maybe it ain't so good, if a man don't have much to offer."

Luis laughed when he wiped off the soap on the razor.

"Maybeso you marry her, Tom?" he asked gently.

Tom shrugged, wondering about it.

"She'd have to be crazy to want me. I've got nothing but an old saddle and an empty belly for her to feed."

"An empty heart too, *verdad?*" he asked.

"Yeah. Empty as a cracked butter churn."

Luis wiped the soap from his face and turned away from the mirror.

"I can see it in her eyes, *compadre*. She is yours. If you want her."

Tom stood up and stretched his arms.

"Ain't much doubt about that, Luis. A man would be a fool not to want a woman like Sara. I can't figure it . . . why she'd want a man like me."

Luis set his sombrero on his head.

"You carry your past too long, my friend," he said. "She does not care that you were once a *pistolero*."

Tom sighed and applied the brush to his cheeks.

"She might," he said thoughtfully, spreading soap over his whiskers, "if I wear that gun again."

The old vaquero paused before he went through the door, watching Tom's face.

"It is never easy to leave the past behind," he said, walking out into a gust of wind.

As soon as Tom entered the cabin Sara ran across the room to fling her arms around his neck. She kissed his cheek and took a step back, her quick smile fading.

"I was so worried about you," she said. "I sent Luis. We thought you might have been thrown . . . or crippled your horse. Luis found your tracks in the dark. He told me about the fence, and the blood. What happened?"

"Another Triangle Bar hand has been killed. Just a boy. I knew him. He died just after I found him . . . told me it was the railroad agents who shot him. I took his body over to the ranch and rode up to Christoval to tell the sheriff. A waste of time. Sheriff Baylor didn't hear a word I said."

Sara dropped her arms and looked thoughtfully past Tom.

"Baylor's new. He made the town a lot of promises last fall. He can't just ignore a murder, can he?"

"He can look the other way," Tom said.

"Any word about Jack?"

Tom took a deep breath, remembering.

"Fever's got him now. The doc says it's bad."

Sara turned away and started for the kitchen, then she stopped, worry in her eyes.

"Somebody has to stop it, Tom," she said. "I'll ride over to Knickerbocker this morning and send a telegraph to the Texas Rangers at Abilene. They won't look the other way."

Tom shook his head.

"You're wrong, Sara. Two Rangers have already been here. One of 'em was Will Dobbs, a man I knew before . . . before

I went to prison. They don't aim to lift a hand to help Johnson."

"Then we can wire the U.S. Marshal. We have to do something," she said impatiently.

He walked over to her and put one arm around her waist.

"I aim to do something," he said softly, gently, wondering where to begin. "The railroad is payin' everybody off so the line can go straight through. There's only one way to put a stop to the trouble."

At first, she didn't understand, he could tell by the look in her eyes.

"Somebody has to silence the railroad's paid guns," he said.

"No, Tom. Not you!"

Tom shrugged and hooked his thumbs in his pockets.

"Nobody else is a match for Odell Pickett," he replied. "Johnson's men are cowboys."

"Oh Tom . . . they could kill you. Even if you win, they'll send you back to prison," she whispered.

He shook his head and stared down at his boots.

"It's a chance I'll have to take. I can't stand by any longer, Sara. The boy . . . he didn't even carry a gun."

When she embraced him her eyes were brimming with tears. She put her face against his chest as he put his arms around her. For a time he held her close to him, trying to think of something to say.

"Maybe it'll work out different," he said.

A moment later she pulled back, fingering a tear from each eye.

"I suppose I should have known it wouldn't work out between the two of us," she said. "Something like this had to come along. I understand, Tom. You've got to do what you think is right."

With the tips of his fingers he wiped a blond curl away

from her forehead, thinking how beautiful she was, how much he felt for her. He had never imagined he could feel this way about a woman . . . never given it a thought after so many years of being alone.

Luis interrupted them, coming through the front door after having fed the horses. Tom let his arms drop. Sara took a step back and gave Luis a smile.

"Breakfast will be ready in a minute," she said, turning for the kitchen, wiping away the last of her tears.

Luis helped stretch the last wire into place while Tom nailed a staple. A hopeful bank of dark clouds held above the northwest horizon. They'd tried to prime the well again and failed at it. The dry summer had dropped the water too low for the pump. They would have to drive the longhorns west, to the river. Unless it rained.

"Maybeso the clouds will be good," Luis said, watching the sky. *"Madre."*

Tom stepped in a stirrup and looked at the clouds. A bolt of lightening appeared, miles to the north. A gust of wind carried the faint scent of rain.

"Maybe," he said when Luis was in the saddle.

They rode off into the wind, hats tilted to keep windblown dust from their eyes. The job sorting the cattle had taken most of the day. It would be dark when they got back to the ranch, well past suppertime. Tom settled in to make the ride, allowing his thoughts to wander back to the meeting with Pickett. Men of his ilk would not leave things idle. Tom knew it, as surely as the next sunrise. Pickett wouldn't run from the fight. His pride wouldn't allow it.

Then he thought about Sara, remembering the moment when he held her in his arms while she cried. He found himself torn by his choices . . . again, the need he felt for

Sara, weighed against the promise he'd given Pickett. Hardly a simple matter to muddle through, one against the other.

He decided, after half an hour of tossing the thing around in his head, that the real choice was in the hands of the Texas and Pacific. He knew he would never back off from the warning he'd given Pickett . . . it wasn't the Spoon way of doing things. If another shot was fired or another fence cut he would ride over to the rail camp and keep his word to Odell. And it wouldn't be easy, not with the kid called Monty and the others to handle. One man against so many would have to play his cards just right, keep any advantage he could find . . . do things careful. Pickett was too smart and too careful to simply draw against him. If Pickett could find a way to get the job done without risking his life, he would do it. All that mattered to men like Pickett was earning his pay. One way or another.

Occupied with such black thoughts, Tom hardly noticed the first raindrops on the wind. A string of dark clouds banked overhead minutes later, popping with distant thunder. Tom took a look skyward when the patter of rain fell on his hat brim. He saw the grin on Luis' face and smelled the rain, taking his mind from the business with Pickett.

"We're liable to float back home," Tom shouted above the wind and thunder.

Luis grinned broadly.

"You can teach the colt to swim," he laughed, spurring to a lope on his grey.

Windblown sheets of rain came from the northwest, swirling around the two men as they rode for the cabin in the dark. Tom was soaked to the skin. Luis' sombrero shed water like a tipped-over bucket. Flashes of lightning showed the way, crackling to a hilltop, often close enough to spook the horses. Trickles of muddy water came from higher ground,

filling the dry washes they crossed. Tom had figured on a
bath anyway. All he needed was a bar of soap.

They rode down to the shed and swung off, standing in a
tiny river of mud. When their saddles were stripped and the
horses put away, Tom followed Luis toward the house, sighting one lit window to guide them through the darkness
between flashes of lightning.

Blackie wagged his tail when they clumped over the boards
across the porch. When Tom opened the door he sensed
something was wrong.

Sara sat in a rocking chair beside the fireplace. An old
double-barreled shotgun lay across her lap. Her face was the
wrong color . . . too white, and her eyes were filled with fear
and worry.

She jumped to her feet and put down the shotgun, then
she ran to Tom's arms and tilted her face to meet his.

"They were here, Tom," she said. "Four men came, from
the railroad. Looking for you."

Tom felt his muscles stiffen.

"Are you okay?" he asked.

Sara nodded quickly.

"Was it Pickett?" he asked, surprised that Odell would
come looking for him.

Her eyes clouded briefly.

"The one who did the talking was young. He said to tell
you Monty Cole was looking for you. He wore two guns. The
others didn't say a word."

Tom understood at once.

"Pickett sent them. When were they here?"

"About noon," she replied, shivering. "There's more,
Tom."

He waited, searching her face until she continued.

"He said . . . he said he'd wait for you at Knickerbocker,
that you would know the place. Please don't go. There were

four of them. We can ride over to the sheriff's office at Christoval in the morning. Let the law handle it, Tom."

Tom let his arms drop from her waist.

"Baylor won't do anything, Sara. They've come for me. I have to go . . . to stop them, before they kill another one of Johnson's cowboys."

"No, Tom," she whispered, pleading with her eyes.

"I have to go," he said softly.

"I will come too," Luis said.

Tom shook his head quickly.

"This isn't your affair, Luis. Stay here. There's work to be done."

Luis took a step closer.

"Four is too many, *compadre*. I will come."

Tom wheeled around to face Luis.

"I said stay. Don't give me any argument," he shouted.

When he stalked out the door his hands were balled into fists. Mindless of the pouring rain, he walked across the yard to the shed and jerked open the door, walking to his warbag hung from a peg above his bunk.

He tossed the bag to one side and struck a match to the lantern. When the wick was right he turned to the bag and dug one hand deep, removing a bundle of leather and iron from the bottom, holding it briefly in the lantern light before he sat down on his bunk.

It had been twelve long years since he'd tied the belt around his waist . . . twelve years of terrible pain and hopelessness that left a scar across his soul. When he uncoiled the leather belt his hands shook, shaking with the pain of so many memories he had tried to forget . . . the men who died in front of his gun, the blood he'd spilled in dusty streets, on the floorboards of saloons, down empty saddles. Tom Spoon had sworn an oath never to wear the gun again

. . . had twelve years to remember the promise he'd made himself.

He pulled the Colt. 44/.40 from the notched holster slowly, lantern light reflected on the metal surface of the gun. His hand closed around the wooden grips. His finger went to the trigger, pausing long enough for him to get the feel of it. He sat rock-still for a time holding the gun, lost in old memories. Then his thumb moved to the hammer. Above the sounds of the storm he heard the click of iron as he cocked the Colt.

He couldn't judge how long he sat with the pistol in his hand before he thumbed open the loading gate, his mind elsewhere, lost in his past. Raindrops pattered down on the rooftop, covering the sound of Luis' boots before he walked into the room. Tom looked up, then he removed six shells from their cartridge loops and thumbed them into the cylinder.

Luis closed the door and stood silently, watching Tom buckle the gunbelt around his waist. Tom tied the rawhide thong around his leg that held the holster in place.

"Gonna be a wet ride to Knickerbocker," Tom said, to make conversation.

"It will be midnight," Luis replied softly.

"They'll wait for me," Tom said, testing the feel of the gun in the holster. "They'll figure I'm coming."

Luis pulled off his sombrero and tossed it on his bunk.

"Remember there are four," he said. "Maybeso they drink too much whiskey."

Tom tried to force a grin.

"Maybe. Keep an eye on things, Luis. Stay close to Sara 'til I get back."

Tom shouldered into his duster coat and walked out into the storm.

"Go with *Dios*," Luis said, the sound of his voice lost in a clap of thunder.

CHAPTER 11

HE pushed the horse harder than a man should, holding a steady lope through the downpour. When he sighted the lights of Knickerbocker the bay was winded, its flanks heaving from the pull through muddy ground.

He slowed to a trot and rode through the outskirts of town, listening to the rattle of his spurs and hooves in mud and water. Then he swung over to a side street and rode up behind the saloon to tie off the bay in the shelter of a live oak tree, loosening the cinch so the gelding could blow.

Several saddled horses stood at the hitchrail, drenched by steady rain, saddles glistening wetly in the light from the windows. One saddle caught his eye . . . decorated with silver conchos around the skirts. It was the mark of a man who fancied himself, likely the gear of the gent called Monty Cole.

Tom walked to the back of the building, mud sucking at his boots, then he opened his duster and swung the coat away from the butt of his gun.

Before he stepped up on the boardwalk he lifted the Colt a little higher in its holster, testing the pull.

His boots made heavy sounds on the wooden planks when he walked down the side of the saloon, spurs rattling. He made no effort to hide his approach, his mouth set in a grim line, ready to make his play. Around the corner, to the batwing doors, he cast a quick look up and down the street.

When he entered the smokey barroom his eyes fell on the

127

group along the bar. Monty Cole looked up when Tom
swung the batwings, a shotglass in one hand.

"Lookee here, boys," Cole said. "The old man showed up
after all. We'd give up on you, Spoon."

Tom stopped, his hand just inches from his gun.

"I came as soon as I heard the invitation," he answered,
glancing at the men on either side of Cole. "Is this just
between you and me? Or are your friends wantin' to try their
luck?"

Cole pushed away from the bar. One hand dangled near
the butt of a pistol as his face went hard.

"I don't need any help with you, old-timer," he said.

Tom tilted his head toward the door.

"Let's take it outside then, son. The barkeep don't want to
spend time moppin' up your blood off his floor."

Cole grinned.

"Suit yourself on it, Spoon," he said.

Tom backed for the door, his eyes on Cole. Thunder
rumbled in the sky above the saloon as Tom cleared the
batwings and then stepped off the boardwalk into the rain.

Water dripped off his hatbrim while Cole took slow steps
to the edge of the porch, then off the boards into the mud.
Tom spread his legs, waiting, watching Cole walk a few paces
into the road.

Men came to the doors to watch the affair, silhouetted by
the lantern light in the saloon. Tom gave them a quick glance,
certain Cole's friends would be gunning for him when the
outcome was clear. If he moved quickly he would have time
to make a dive behind the tethered horses at the hitchrail.
But first, there was the business with Monty Cole.

Cole spread his feet and hunkered down, hands poised
above his pistols.

"Any time, old man," he said, grinning when he said it.

"I'll let you take the first pull," Tom answered, matching Cole's grin with his own.

"My pleasure," the man said, his right hand dipping toward his gun.

Tom's hand closed around the gunbutt, a practiced move, his thumb working the hammer back. Before Cole's gun was clear, before he had any chance of a shot, Tom pulled the trigger.

The slug hit the middle of Cole's chest. Dark fluid exploded from his shirtfront, knocking him back. Deep mud held Cole's boots when he tried to keep himself from falling. The force of Tom's bullet slammed Cole to the muddy street, one pistol falling at his side in a watery wagon rut, the other still clamped in Cole's hand.

Tom swung the Colt toward the batwings, crouched for a lunge behind frightened horses at the rail. He knew Cole was as good as dead, worrying about the others, ready for them to make their play, waiting for the gunshots from the doorway.

He was surprised when he saw open palms above the batwings, hands lifted toward the sky, empty. It made no sense that Cole's friends were empty-handed with their arms over their heads. Tom saw it, not believing what he saw, puzzled by the silence from the saloon.

The answer followed the men out to the boardwalk. Luis held a pistol at the men's backs, shoving them out into the rain in front of his gun.

"Luis," he said, too surprised to think of anything else to say.

"I follow you, *compadre*," he said, grinning below his big sombrero. "*Madre*, but you ride that horse hard. I have trouble staying up. I come in the back door. These *pendejos* don't hear me," he chuckled.

Tom was angry and relieved at the same time. He lowered

the Colt and took his eyes off the men on the porch, stepping over to Monty Cole.

Raindrops splattered over Cole's face, washing away mud. Cole's eyes were open, wrinkling at the corners as he fought the pain in his chest. Rain spilled from Tom's hatbrim while he stood over the body, rain he hardly noticed, his mind adrift in old memories.

"Hell of a way to learn a lesson, son," he said, more to himself than Cole. "I reckon your kind never learns."

Cole's pain-ridden gaze fell on Tom. Now, too late, there was fear in his eyes.

Tom turned away and walked through deepening mud to the boardwalk. A bolt of lightning brightened the sky briefly.

The three gunhands shifted uneasily under Tom's stare, arms lifted, glancing nervously at each other, then back to Tom.

"You boys unbuckle those gunbelts," Tom said. "Do it slow. Two of you get Cole and carry him to the porch. If there's a doctor in town we'll send somebody to fetch him. If any one of you so much as scratches your ear wrong, I'll kill you."

Heavy gunbelts fell to the boards. Then two stepped into the mud, one eye on Tom, lifting Monty Cole by his feet and shoulders, struggling through watery ruts to the porch.

When Cole was stretched out on the boards they stood back.

Tom swung his gun on the other of the three.

"Get on your horse," Tom said evenly. "High-tail it for that railroad camp and tell Odell Pickett he'll be next. Tell him he's had my last warning. One more piece of trouble comes to the Triangle Bar and I'll ride over and kill him."

The man nodded quickly. Without a slicker or a duster he swung off the porch and ran to a horse tied at the rail, hurrying to mount, then spurring hard away from the saloon, his horse scattering mud from its path.

"If there's a lawman in Knickerbocker, somebody go get him," Tom said, holstering his gun. "Luis, take these two inside."

When they walked into the saloon, all was quiet. Luis aimed the two gunmen for vacant chairs, standing over them with his pistol. Tom walked past silent patrons to the bar.

"Pour me a whiskey," he said.

A whiskered barman obliged Tom with a shotglass, poured to the rim. Tom took the drink and tossed it back.

"We ain't got any law in Knickerbocker," the barkeep said, his eyes fixed on Tom. "U.S. Marshal from Abilene, or the Rangers handle things here. Town's too small."

Tom shook his head.

"No doctor either," the man went on. "Closest is over at Christoval. No need sending for Doc Spence . . . the feller you shot is same as dead."

"Send a wire to the Marshal's office in the morning," Tom said, his back to the bar. "Tell him what you saw. I'll be at the Clay Ranch if he wants to hear my side. Reckon I'll let these two gents go . . . I'll keep their guns."

Luis dropped his pistol in his holster. Tom walked over to the table and gave the pair a hard look.

"My advice is, you boys ride clear of this country," he said. "Railroad pay may be good, but it ain't good enough to be worth dyin' for. If you strap on a gun again against the Triangle Bar, you'll wind up like Monty Cole. Follow my advice and clear out."

They came to their feet slowly, uncertain.

"I seen enough," one said, glancing toward the other. "I don't want no part of you, Tom Spoon."

Luis followed them to the batwings, keeping a careful eye on them until they were in their saddles and off into the rainstorm. When Luis turned away from the doors Tom let out a breath and ordered a pair of whiskies. Luis joined him at the bar to toss down drinks.

"Mind if I ask a question?" the barman asked, wiping a rag over his bar.

When Tom shrugged, the man continued.

"How come you let that bunch push you around before?" he asked. "I ain't never seen a feller so fast with a six-gun."

Tom considered his answer for a time, toying with his empty glass.

"I make it a practice to mind my own business," he said. "They let their business get mixed up with mine this time."

The rains brought an overnight freshness to the grasses, new life to the yellowed stalks they rode past. Tom let the bay have his head, riding cross-country looking for bunches of cattle in the east pastures. The pump still wouldn't prime, thus the cattle had to be pushed toward the river until the water table came higher in the well. Things smelled clean, as Tom rode the ranch pastures. It seemed the rain had scrubbed the dry land and made it more presentable. Dewy droplets clung to the blades of grass, sparkling in the sunlight.

He reined in beside Luis on a hilltop. A handful of cows grazed in the distance, meandering over the hills behind an old bull.

"Pretty sight, ain't it?" Tom asked.

Luis said nothing, only a shake of his head.

"Let's bunch 'em and head them for the river."

The riders split to get the cattle started in the right direction, driving an occasional stray back in the herd. Tom found himself alone with his thoughts, sorting through a mixture of feelings over recent events. Time spent off to himself in a saddle allowed him the chance to get things straight . . . he could have a talk with himself and set things in order.

When he put the gunbelt away the day before, the morning he and Luis arrived back at the ranch, he was in a black mood over it . . . shooting Monty Cole. When it was done, he felt no satisfaction over the affair, even though it stood a chance of ending the trouble for the Triangle Bar. Down in his gut he figured the trouble would shift his way, either from Pickett, or the law, maybe both. Either way, it would end the peace he had known working for Sara. Last night, after supper as he stood in the darkness beside a corral, he'd given thought to packing his gear to head west. It was the woman, he decided, that kept him from it . . . the way he felt about her, the way she made him feel.

When he told her what had happened at Knickerbocker she put her arms around him . . . she never said a word about it at all. He knew then he could never simply ride off and leave her, not so long as he had a choice.

Thus he decided he would play the cards he was dealt and wait. His feelings for the woman gave him no selection.

When the cattle were in sight of the river Luis joined him on a ridge to watch the longhorns settle, following the bull to water. The rains had swollen the Concho to bankfull, a natural barrier that would hold Circle C cows where they belonged.

"It'll be a good fall," Tom observed. "The calves will get fat now. With a good stand of winter grass, we'll be in good shape until spring."

Luis agreed with a shake of his head.

"Then you will stay, *compadre?*" he asked, watching Tom.

"I was plannin' on it. What made you guess otherwise?"

"When you killed the *pistolero,* I think maybeso you leave in a hurry," Luis answered.

Tom shook his head.

"Not so long as I've got a choice, Luis. Maybe things will quiet down. I reckon you know how I feel about Sara. If she wants me around, I aim to stay."

Something about the old man's face wasn't right, Tom decided as he gazed toward him. For a time Luis was silent, making a study of the cows in the distance.

"When one man dies, *compadre,* there will be another who wants revenge," he said.

Tom swung a look toward the horizon.

"I've been figurin' on it, too," he replied. "Got no choice but to wait and see . . . but I'm stayin' . . . if I can."

"Bueno," Luis said, adopting his usual habit of breaking into Spanish when a word escaped him. "It is good. The woman is like my own daughter. She has eyes for you, Tom. It will hurt her if you go."

"The only place I'm liable to go is jail," he said after a minute of thought. "I figure that's up to the railroad and the law. Folks in Knickerbocker saw what happened . . . saw Cole go for his gun first. Sometimes that ain't enough. I did twelve years in a box proving that."

Tom reined off the ridge, wanting an end to the reminders of a past he tried to forget. Luis rode silently beside him back to the ranch as dusk came over the hilly land.

At supper, Sara smiled for him and asked about the well.

"It won't prime just yet," he said. "Give it a day or two and we'll be back in business. Takes some time for the water to rise."

She ran a hand through her hair, touching a pink ribbon that held her curls in place.

"Give those calves two months and we'll have plenty of beef to drive to Abilene," she said. "The cows will make the winter in good shape. Looks like a good year, Tom."

He laughed when he thought about the cracks in the wall of the shed.

"Me and Luis are liable to freeze stiff in the bunk house," he replied.

Her eyes fell on his, holding him with a look.

"Then you'll stay out the winter?" she asked softly.

"Never figured otherwise," he said, grinning.

She reached across the table to touch his hand, and when she did it his cheeks felt hot with Luis watching.

"I'm glad," she replied. "We need you around here."

He was aboard the paint colt when he first glimpsed the two riders. The young gelding moved around the corral under the pressure of the rein, holding promise of making a good ranch horse with a soft mouth and an easy way of going. The two men who crossed the ridge above the ranch came at a trot, forcing Tom out of the saddle from worry.

"Two men come," Luis said from a late evening shadow near the shed.

"I see 'em," Tom replied uneasily, watching the riders approach.

He tied the paint to the fence and went through the gate, wondering if he should hurry to the shed for his gunbelt. Visitors would likely mean trouble, after the affair at Knickerbocker. He'd been expecting it all along.

When the men were close, Tom recognized one in the fading light. Will Dobbs rode slump-shouldered atop a buckskin, his face hidden below his hat, only the handlebar mustache visible in the shadow from his hat brim.

"Evenin', Tom," he said when the buckskin came to a halt.

The Ranger's eyes flickered around the place briefly, to the front porch when Sara came out, banging the door. Then his gaze went back to Tom. A deputy with a star pinned to his chest sat beside Dobbs, the same gent who was with Dobbs at Christoval.

"Need to talk," he said, resting a hand on his saddlehorn,

the other near his gun. "Investigatin' the killing over at the Knickerbocker saloon. Folks say it was you done the shootin' the other day."

Tom hooked his thumbs in his pockets and gave a nod.

"They're right about it, Will. Feller went by the name of Monty Cole. Didn't wait around to see if he was dead, but I'll take your word for it."

Dobbs hardened his face, working his mustache.

"Cole was a peace officer, Tom. A deputy of the Texas and Pacific Railroad."

Tom shrugged, to say it made no difference.

"Went for his gun first, Will," Tom answered, knowing it wouldn't matter to Will Dobbs.

Dobbs sat his horse, silent.

"That ain't the way some folks tell it," Dobbs replied after a time.

"You heard wrong," Tom said, growing tired of the banter.

In the silence that followed they took stock of each other, neither willing to look the other way.

"Puts me in a bad position," Dobbs said when the silence grew uncomfortable.

"Ask the bartender," Tom said when he could think of nothing better. "He saw the whole thing."

Dobbs made no move when he replied.

"There's others saw it different, Tom."

"Railroad men, would be my guess. Cole had three friends with him. Likely you heard from them."

"Didn't get their names. A couple said you pulled first."

"It didn't happen that way. Cole swung by this ranch and said to come. I rode up and obliged him. He wanted to try his luck. Thought he was faster, I reckon."

"Appears he weren't so fast," Dobbs observed dryly. "I figured you were too old to be much with a gun any more, Spoon. A man gets slower with time."

Tom shifted his weight, waiting for Dobbs to make his point. Then he heard spurs behind him and swung a look back. Luis came from the shed, wearing his gunbelt.

"The other *hombre* drew first," Luis said, halting when he was some distance away. "I was there."

Dobbs tossed an impatient look at Luis.

"It figures you'd take Spoon's side."

Luis spread his palms while Sara hurried off the porch.

"I was there, *señor*," he said again.

Sara stopped beside Tom and looked up at Will Dobbs.

"The four of them came here, just like Tom said," she said stiffly, "and what Luis told you is the truth. He told me about it. I've known Judge Haney since we built this place. He knows Luis. If it comes down to a trial, the judge knows we wouldn't lie about what happened. You'll have a hard time making a case against Tom."

Dobbs was irritated . . . made it plain by the look on his face.

"Tom Spoon is an outlaw, ma'am. Maybe he hasn't told you. He did a stretch in state prison for killing a man over in Waco."

"He told me," she said, defiance in her voice.

Dobbs fingered his reins.

"That ain't all, lady. Tom Spoon is a paid killer. He's killed more men than I care to count. Could be he hasn't told you everything."

Sara hardly batted an eye. "That doesn't matter to me. He does his job around here. He earns his pay."

Dobbs was left with few choices. He gave Tom a look and took a breath.

"I'll look into it some more," he said.

"You do that," Sara snapped, placing her hands on her hips. "While you're at it I'll ride over to San Angelo and have a word with Judge Haney. Luis can ride along and tell the judge what he saw. While I'm there I plan to mention this business with the railroad. Maybe if I tell him what's been happening to the men over at the Triangle Bar, he'll send down a U.S. Marshal to look into it."

Dobb's hands tightened. It was plain he hadn't figured on such a thing from Sara Clay.

"That's your affair, lady," he said. Then he lifted his reins and got ready to ride.

"Didn't figure it, Tom," he said, like he was surprised by what he heard. "Times have changed since you went to prison. Ain't much call for a gunhand any more. Old man like you, with a reputation bad as yours, ain't hardly welcome most places. Not much need for a shootist nowadays. Things are different now."

Tom didn't give an answer. Dobbs reined away and hit a trot beside his deputy, riding into the last rays of sunlight across the landscape.

"Tell it to the railroad," Tom said, to himself when Dobbs was out of earshot. "Ask them why they need Odell Pickett."

CHAPTER 12

SARA wouldn't hear of it. Tom's argument fell on deaf ears at the supper table.

"I'm going," she said, directing a look toward both men. "We need staples, and there's too much work to be done around here to spare either one of you. I can drive the wagon over by myself . . . I've done it before a hundred times. I can take the Winchester. I know how to use it."

Tom shook his head again against the idea.

"Things are different just now, Sara," he said. "With all this trouble brewing, it ain't safe for you to try it alone."

She stiffened in her seat.

"The subject is closed, Tom. I'm going in the morning. I'll buy supplies in Angelo and drop by for a word with Judge Haney. The trip'll take two days."

Tom looked helplessly at Luis.

"Will she listen to you?" he asked.

Luis grinned sheepishly around a biscuit. "No, *compadre*. This woman is different. You waste your words."

Tom's belly tightened with worry, wondering if Pickett or his men would harm Sara.

"I'm against it," he said, figuring he would have better luck arguing with the black dog.

"Something has to be done, Tom," she said. "Any fool can see those Texas Rangers are looking for a way to make trouble for you. From what you've told me, Joe Baylor is on the take from the railroad, too. Crooked lawmen should be

139

stopped. Judge Haney is an honest man. He'll know what to do."

"It isn't just the law," Tom said. "The folks over in town want the railroad, too . . . it means more business for everybody. You ain't gonna be very popular, taking Jack Johnson's side."

"I couldn't care less," she said hotly. "Jack's within his rights. A railroad can't make someone sell land. The whole south end of Jack's ranch will be useless without water for his livestock. He can't graze it."

Tom let it drop, facing certain defeat. Luis was right, this woman was different, perhaps one reason why Tom cared for her in a way he'd be hard pressed to explain.

After supper they walked out on the porch. Luis left for the shed, leaving Tom alone with Sara beneath a starry sky in a cool westerly breeze.

"Don't worry about me," she said, taking his hand. "I can handle myself. Since Bill died I've been on my own out here. I'm not just a frilly woman who can't take care of myself."

He stared down at the soft lines of her face and tightened his hand around hers.

"I just don't want anything to happen to you, Sara," he said. "I . . . I guess I never felt like this before about somebody else. It don't come real natural for me . . . can't get used to it just yet. Give me a little time."

She swung around and pressed both palms against his cheeks.

"I think you know I feel the same way about you," she whispered. "When you rode off to Knickerbocker in the storm I couldn't help myself . . . I started crying. I love you, Tom."

She stood on her toes and kissed him lightly.

"I love you, too," he said hoarsely, the words strange and somehow wrong, coming from his mouth. "There ain't much about me for a woman to care about. All my life I've been a drifter. Never did stay in one place long enough to get my hat hung. You know most of what there is about my past. I've killed enough men to fill a boneyard . . . been to prison for a dozen years. You ain't picked the best from the herd when you got me."

She rested her head against his chest and put her arms around him.

"I don't care about your past," she said softly. "All I care about is what happens from here on."

Tom touched her shoulders gently. He looked up at the sky, questioning his good fortune, suddenly afraid it was too good to last.

"My past may not be done with me just yet," he said. "The business with the railroad . . ."

He didn't finish the remark, figuring the less was said about it, the better.

"I know you'll do what you have to do," she replied. "If I talk to Judge Haney, maybe he can stop it."

She kissed him again and took his hand, leading him to the door.

Sara drove off in the buckboard at sunup. Tom watched her drive over the ridge above the ranch, then he turned quickly to Luis.

"Follow her," he said. "Stay out of sight. She'll be mad as a nest of hornets, but I can't let her go alone. I can handle things while you're gone."

Luis swung in his saddle.

Tom took quick notice that Luis wore his gun.

"Do not worry, *compadre*," he said. "She will be safe with me."

Before Luis rode away from the shed, he swept a look across the eastern horizon.

"Be very careful, my friend," he said, then he spurred the grey north behind the tracks of the wagon.

Tom cinched the bay and rode west toward the river, his mind on Sara, paying little attention to the trail he followed. Last night, as he held Sara in his arms, he'd come to a decision of sorts. He would keep his nose out of business that wasn't his no matter how he felt about the right or the wrong of it. The years he had left would be spent working this ranch minding his own affairs. It was his plan to ride over to the Concho and throw his gunbelt and pistol in the middle of the river, so he would never be tempted again to take a hand in things. When Sara got back he would do it. He made himself that promise as he rode across Circle C land.

With his mind occupied, he checked the grazing herds until midafternoon, watching the calve's flanks fill on renewed grass after the rains. Fingers of green color had begun to climb up from the roots of the grasses, holding promise of a good fall roundup.

At dark he found himself alone in the kitchen, fixing his own supper on the iron cookstove. He was all thumbs as he went about it, spilling this and that, burning a piece of meat to a cinder in Sara's skillet.

Later, he took a walk around the ranch, checking the corrals and the windmill trough, satisfied that things were as they should be. Horses grazed on stacks of hay inside the pens. Blackie followed him around, making his own study of chicken roosts and distant hilltops where coyotes howled at the sky.

He lit the lantern inside the shed and lay across his bunk, thinking about Sara . . . and the ranch, all the things he'd grown comfortable with since he came to the Circle C.

"Wouldn't be a bad life at all," he thought, considering the prospects idly. "Better than bein' on the move, wondering if the next gunfight would be my last. You got lucky with the kid Monty Cole," he told himself. "If Luis hadn't shown up when he did, you might have cashed in your chips with the rest of Pickett's men."

He drifted off to sleep some time later, fully dressed with his boots hung off the edge of his bunk.

Dawn put him back in the saddle for another try at the windmill pump along the east fence. As he rode he wondered about the chances of finding more cut fence. Busted wires would mean he'd be forced into a move against Odell Pickett and the railroad, a black thought now that he'd made his choice to stay at the Circle C with Sara, no matter what. Silently, he hoped the fence was strung tight when he rode up on it.

Toward noon he was in sight of the fence. Barbed wires were stretched as far as he could see in both directions. When he swung down at the windmill he had more good luck. One tin cup of water started the flow from the length of pipe. The cattle could be driven back to the good east pastures. Things were beginning to take on a better look.

It was dusky dark when he put the bay in the corral and started for the cabin. When Blackie gave a low growl he was puzzled by it, until he saw the rider crossing a ridge, aimed for the ranch. Tom stood, watching the horseman with a knot forming in his belly.

As the rider drew near, Tom recognized him. One of Odell Pickett's men trotted a sorrel gelding past the first corral, a gun tied around his waist. Tom hurried for the shed to get his gunbelt. One of the men he'd let ride away from the affair at Knickerbocker had come back to try his luck with Tom.

Tom met him in the yard, ready for trouble, watching the gunman's hand.

"Pickett wants to see you, Spoon," the man said when his horse was reined down. "Said to bring your gun."

Tom gave a slight nod, to say he understood.

"Tell him I'll be there. Tell him I couldn't figure why he waited so long."

"I'll tell him," the man replied. "Be seein' you at the railroad camp."

"I'll be there," Tom said, watching the rider turn his horse.

CHAPTER 13

HE checked rein on a bluff above the rail camp and let the bay gather wind. A noonday sun baked the prairie below the bluff. Hot wind gusted around him, kicking little plumes of dust skyward. Below, the rows of canvas tents reflected sunlight. He cast a look toward the rail cars where Pickett would be waiting.

On the ride over he thought about many things, knowing a draw with Pickett would not be easy. Odell was much older and wiser than Monty Cole . . . experienced in the finer things that made the difference between life and death with a quick draw. Years before, the advantage had belonged to Tom. It would be different now.

He tested the pull of his Colt, wondering about the outcome, thinking about Sara. He was betting everything on a talent he hadn't used for years. The draw against Cole had been child's play.

He thought back to the note he'd left Sara, propped against the sugar bowl atop the table. Crudely worded, he told her how much he loved her, hoping he'd spelled enough words right so she would know what he felt . . . how much he cared. The note was a bet to cover the odds, just in case Pickett's luck was better than his. If Pickett killed him, he wanted Sara to know he had no choice but to come at Pickett's invitation. Spoon blood wouldn't allow anything else. There was no other way.

"Well, old man," he said to himself aloud, his voice carried away on a gust of wind. "You've been down this road before. If you live through it this time, it'll damn sure be the last."

He touched a spur to the bay's ribs and started off the bluff, wondering how it would go. A man without choices, he put his mind on the task and got ready for his last gunfight, one way or another.

He trotted past the tents, dust rolling away from his horse's hooves, drawing closer to the rail cars. A tiny knot of men was formed around the back of the last car, watching him approach. He counted five. One was the gent named Carruthers. One was Odell Pickett, slouched against the side of the car.

Before Tom halted the bay, Pickett straightened and took steps toward Tom. Pickett was dressed in his black suit, his hat lowered to shield his face from the sun.

Tom drew rein fifty yards from Pickett.

"Get down, Tom," Pickett said, noticing Tom's glance toward the other men. "This is just between you and me," his voice like a rasp across hot iron.

Tom left his gunhand free as he swung down from the bay. He let the reins drop to the ground, his eyes locked on Pickett as the horse wandered away.

Wind blew sand and dust between them, yet neither blinked. A cluster of gandy dancers and rail hands started to form to one side of the spot, watching the men face each other.

"Rode over quick as I could, Odell," Tom said. "Had a windmill to fix first. Been wonderin' why you hadn't paid me a call."

It was the casual sound of Tom's voice that made Pickett stiffen his right hand.

"Didn't leave me much choice, Tom. Made my deputies look like greenhorns. You know I can't turn my back on it."

"I figured," Tom sighed. "Been waitin' for this to come."

Pickett tried to force a grin.

"A man has to earn his money," he said, softer than before.

"There's another way, Odell. Let it alone. Ride away from it.

Pickett shook his head slowly.

"You know I can't do that, Spoon. There's reputations at stake here . . . yours and mine."

Tom watched Pickett's hand, ready for a pull.

"Time in a prison cell taught me a thing or two, Odell," Tom said carefully. "I couldn't spend my reputation behind bars. I was just another feller breakin' rocks."

Pickett shook his head.

"If I run from you, Spoon, I'd never make another payday," he said.

"Then you'll never make another payday either way, Odell," Tom said quietly. "I'm faster."

There was the briefest of moments when Pickett seemed uncertain . . . he said so with his eyes.

"You was once, Tom. It's been a few years."

As the words left his mouth, Pickett went for his gun. Tom saw his fingers close around his gunbutt.

It happened slowly, when time is measured with blood, mere fractions of a second that spell the difference between men who live by the gun. Pickett's hand came up filled with deadly iron, aimed for Tom's chest. Tom heard the cocking hammer. Time stood still, frozen like rain in a winter storm as Tom brought the .44/.40 up for a shot.

One gun exploded, filling the silence between them. A finger of flame came from one barrel at almost the same instant the second gun fired. One shot found its mark a heartbeat ahead of the other, sending the second shot wide.

Blue gunsmoke billowed across the yards separating the men. One man staggered back as the shots echoed.

Odell Pickett turned. His polished boots worked to hold

him upright. A shower of blood fell from the hole in his belly. One hand came up to stop the flow, the other relaxed its grip on the gun.

Tom watched Pickett struggle to stay on his feet, reminded of others who danced the same steps in front of his gun. Pickett swayed, then the pistol fell from his hand, thumping beside him in the dirt.

Slowly, Pickett sank to his knees, holding his wound with a pair of bloody hands, his eyes on Tom. Tom watched without feeling, holding the Colt leveled in front of him.

Color drained quickly from Pickett's face. His mouth worked but no words came out. A dark stain spread down Pickett's vest, below the badge, spilling over his gunbelt.

It seemed forever that Pickett held himself off the ground, before he fell forward on his face limply. One boot shook, rattling a spur rowel.

Tom swung his gun toward the men around Carruthers. Not a hand was lifted toward a gun. Harding Carruthers stared down at Pickett's body, blinking, chewing one fleshy lip.

A silence spread over the rail camp. The work crews stood to Tom's right, unmoving, staring down at Pickett. A cloud of dust swept over the spot, whistling past.

Carruthers took the first step . . . backward, inching his way toward the rail car.

"Hold still," Tom said above the wind, following Carruthers with his gunbarrel. "I'll have a word with you."

Carruthers froze, swallowing, watching Tom . . . and the gun. Tom walked over to the spot where Pickett lay, halting long enough to cast a glance toward the other gunmen.

"Drop the belts again, boys," he said. "Seems we've done this before."

Three gunbelts fell to the ground, then empty hands were

raised. When Tom was satisfied he lifted a boot and shoved Odell Pickett over on his back.

Chalky dust clung to the black coat and vest, to the gun-fighter's face and arms. Pale blue eyes stared up at the sky, frozen wide with the nearness of death, unseeing. A trickle of blood came from the wound, running to one side, pooling in the caliche dust.

Tom faced Harding Carruthers, letting the Colt dangle in his right hand. There was no sound until Tom spoke, only the whisper of dry wind.

"This ends it, Carruthers," Tom said. "Run your goddamn rails around Johnson, or the next man to die over that piece of ground will be you."

The overfed face nodded quickly.

"A U.S. Marshal is on his way from Abilene," Tom went on. "Could be he'll charge you with murder. It was your money got those men killed."

Then Tom's jaw clamped down hard when he turned to the other gunmen. He walked away from Carruthers to stand in front of the three men, a hard set to his mouth when he spoke.

"Get mounted, boys," he said. "If I ever lay eyes on a one of you again I swear I'll blow you right outa your boots."

One turned ahead of the rest, hurrying for a line of picketed horses. Tom stood his ground until the men were in their saddles away from the rail camp, then he walked to the bay and gathered his reins.

When he swung up he took a last look at Odell Pickett, now only a dusty body sprawled beside the rail car, his chest stilled. Tom touched the brim of his hat, a salute to the last man to die by the hand of Tom Spoon.

CHAPTER 14

THE ride back to the ranch seemed longer than he remembered it. A thousand thoughts rattled around inside his head at once, most of them centered around Sara. Trotting over the empty miles, he wondered how Sara would feel about him when he told her the truth . . . when he told her what he'd done. A knot formed in his belly, glancing down at his gun.

A mile from the railroad camp he had taken off his gunbelt and hung it around his saddlehorn, trying to push aside the memory of the gunfight with Pickett. But it wouldn't leave him alone, seeing it over and over again in his mind's eye. Gradually, he was forced to admit there was a part of himself he didn't know as well as he figured. All those years of promising himself that he was finished with gunplay hadn't been enough to stop him when the chips were down, and the thought troubled him. He had no choice but to admit that there was a side to him he couldn't control. Worst was, he worried that Sara would feel the same way and want no part of him . . . want no part of a killer.

"Damn it all, Spoon," he muttered under his breath, angry at himself for losing control.

When he crested a rise that gave him a view of the cabin, his mouth went dry.

"You've got yourself some tall talking to do," he said aloud, hurrying his horse with a spur.

Blackie met him in the yard, wagging his tail. Before he had a leg swung over his saddle, the cabin door opened. Sara

151

came out on the porch. It was easy to see that she'd been crying.

"Tom," she said, choking back tears, then she ran off the porch and threw her arms around his neck, searching his face.

He pulled off his hat and bent to kiss her.

"Where have you been?" she cried, her eyes brimming with tears. "When we got back, the shed was empty and your horse was gone . . . then I found your note and I . . ."

She didn't finish, burying her face against his chest.

He stroked her hair, wondering where to begin.

"It's a long story, Sara. Hear me out all the way, before you make up your mind about what I've done."

She looked into his eyes.

"I don't care what you did, Tom. You don't have to tell me," she whispered hoarsely. "You came back, and that's all that matters to me."

"I killed a man, Sara. I rode over to the rail camp and killed one of their hired guns. It adds up to two . . . the gunman at Knickerbocker, and now there's Pickett. They're liable to send me back to prison."

"No. Nobody's going to send you away for helping Jack Johnson fight the railroad. I talked to Judge Haney, and so did Luis. A U.S. Marshal is being sent down to look into things. When he finds out the truth . . ."

Something stirred in Tom's chest. Gazing down at Sara, he knew he could never high-tail it for Mexico or leave the ranch for the New Mexico territory. He loved the woman standing beside him. He would stay and see things through.

"I was afraid you'd want no part of me when I told you what I'd done. I couldn't help myself, Sara. I couldn't stand by and let it pass. I guess there's a side to me that I can't change."

"It's over, Tom," she whispered, tightening her arms

around his neck. "We can go on with our lives. Leave it in the past."

"Seems I can't shake my old shadow," Tom sighed, feeling Sara's tears on his shirtfront. "I swore I wouldn't let it happen, but it did. I reckon there are some things you ought to know about me, so you'll know what you're getting yourself into. Walk along with me, and listen to what I've got to say."

He pulled her arms from his neck and took her hand.

"You don't have to, Tom. I don't care about your past."

Tom gazed toward the horizon.

"I figure I need to get it off my chest." Tom sighed. "I want you to know who I am. Then you can decide."

He started toward the corrals, squeezing Sara's tiny hand. His horse followed along with the pull on its reins.

"I do a better job of talking when my feet are on the move," Tom chuckled. "Sounds silly, but I never was much good at makin' speeches."

When they were away from the barns, Tom halted on a grassy knoll overlooking the shallow valley.

"Before I went to prison, I was a gunfighter," Tom said, staring off at nothing, remembering his past. "In my time, I killed more than just a handful of men. I was a paid shootist, Sara. A hired killer."

Tom swallowed. His tongue had gone dry as sand.

"I told myself I always tried to be on the right side of things. I never took a job that didn't suit me, where I was taking a hand against folks who couldn't defend themselves. I believed that, back then. I suppose it was a way to keep my conscience quiet. And I never pulled on another man first, not once in all those years carrying a gun. I don't reckon it matters now, but that's the way I done it."

"You told me about your past once before," Sara said, "and I told you then it didn't matter to me. I understand why you used a gun this time. It doesn't change the way I feel about you, Tom."

He felt her fingers tighten around his palm. He took his eyes from the distant hills to study Sara's face.

"I wanted you to know what kind of cold-jawed bronc I am," he said softly. "I took it as long as I could. I turned my back on a friend when I rode away from Jack Johnson's place, but Pickett and his bunch kept pushing me. I figured I could look the other way, but I guessed wrong."

"I don't care," Sara whispered. "All I care about is the way you feel about me."

A lump came to Tom's throat. He knew what he wanted to say, hoping the words would line up just right on his tongue before they spilled from his mouth.

"I love you, Sara," he said. He'd said it once before and when he did, it didn't sound quite right. This time, he liked the way the words echoed in his ears.

"I love you, too, Tom Spoon," she said softly, letting go of his hand to put her arms around him.

He kissed her, lightly, gently, trying not to crush her when he tightened his arms around her.

They stood in each other's arms for a time. Dusk settled over the prairie hills, painting shadows beneath the mesquites and cholla. Off in the distance a coyote barked, signaling the coming of dark. A few yards away, Blackie whimpered, reminding Tom that they had an audience. Tom took his arms from Sara's shoulders, wondering if old Luis was watching from the shed.

"There are chores to be done," he said, glancing toward the corrals. "I reckon I forgot I was still hired on at this spread."

Sara touched his cheek with her fingertips.

"You don't have to be a hired hand around here any longer," she replied, smiling. "Think about it, Tom."

A smile formed on his lips. He understood what Sara meant. He tried to think of the right thing to say, the way he wanted the words to come out, looking off while he gathered his thoughts. Then his eyes came to rest on the gunbelt hanging from his saddlehorn, reminding him of some unfinished business.

"Let's take a ride," he said, taking Sara's arm. "Don't ask me any questions just yet. I'll explain when we get where we're going."

He helped her into the saddle, then he swung up behind and put his arms around her waist.

"Head for the river," he said, feeling the softness of her hair against his face as the horse started off the hill.

"Why are we going to the river?" she asked, reining west.

He did not answer her, watching the horizon as a pale moon appeared above a ridge, bathing the silent prairie in soft, silvery light.

They rode over a crest above the Concho, then down a gentle slope to the muddy current, still full to the banks from the recent rains. When they reached the water's edge, Tom swung down and removed his gunbelt from the saddlehorn.

He stood silently on the riverbank for a time, feeling Sara's eyes on his back. The weight of the .44/.40 grew heavier in his hands.

"What's wrong, Tom?" she asked.

His answer made her catch her breath. He tossed the gunbelt high in the air above the silvery flow of the Concho, then there was a splash when it dropped out of sight beneath the surface.

They sat on the long front porch overlooking the corrals where he first rode the big blue stud, rocked back in wicker chairs, passing the whiskey back and forth. Tom could hear

Sara's voice through an open window, chattering with Margaret Johnson.

"I've been thinkin'," Tom said, toying with his empty glass. "Wondering if you'd sell me Big Blue and some mares."

"I'll give 'em to you, Tom," Jack replied. "I owe you. Take the stud and have your pick of the mares. Money can't buy what you did for me."

Tom watched the rancher's face. Jack's color was better now. The doc said he was healing fast.

"I'll think on it," Tom said, "but I'd rather pay. Me an' Sara will have a good calf crop to sell. We can pay. We decided to raise a few good horses at the Circle C. I can't think of a better stud to sire our colts than Big Blue. Set a price on him, and a price for the mares."

Jack shook his head and waved the idea away.

"You're the only cowboy ever to ride Blue to a standstill, so it would be fittin' that you owned him. He's yours for the taking. I won't take a cent of your money. I guess I'd ask one favor of you . . . don't break the old horse to a saddle. You'll think I've gone soft in the head, but if a horse can have such a thing as pride, ol' Blue is proud of the bronc stompers he's dumped from a saddle in his lifetime. I owe the horse that much. I'd ask that you let Blue hang on to his pride."

Tom chuckled, remembering the fierce bronc ride aboard the grey.

"Maybe I'm soft, too," Tom said, "but it wouldn't seem right to cinch a saddle on him now. There's some horses wasn't meant to be rode. I figure Blue has earned the right to be free from a cowboy's weight."

Then Jack got a look of amusement on his face.

"I've got a better idea, Tom. You could take a spotted stud colt sired by my Palouse stallion Chinook. A Palouse makes the best cowhorse you ever tied a saddle on and they're mighty damn pretty to look at to boot."

Tom shook his head and sipped whiskey, grinning when he passed the bottle back to Jack.

"If it's all the same to you, I'll take the grey. I'm kind'a like Slim Willis on the subject . . . I'd just as soon not be seen ridin' a two-colored horse."

They laughed about it as Sara and Margaret came out on the porch.

"Supper is ready," Sara said, coming over to Tom to place a hand on his shoulder. "What are the two of you laughing about?"

"Two-colored horses," Tom replied, taking Sara's hand.

"And women," Jack added with a wink. "We've come to the conclusion that there ain't a man wearin' boots who understands a woman's ideas on things. Just this morning, Margaret said I wasn't able to ride a horse just yet. I told her I was able to sit this chair, so I could damn sure sit a saddle."

Margaret frowned.

"If you could ride as well as you cuss, I'd have no objection to the notion," she said. "You're a hard-headed old fool for thinking you could ride all the way to the Circle C. The doctor said to take it easy until your wound healed, husband. Now come inside and eat your supper."

"Women," Jack sighed, lifting gingerly from the chair. "Come on in, Tom. It's a waste of good time to stay out here arguing with a woman."

Before they left the porch, Jack stopped to gaze toward the barns.

"Mighty glad to have you folks as neighbors," Jack said wistfully. "We're gonna have some peace in this valley for a change, and we owe it all to Tom Spoon."

Tom stiffened. In the weeks since the gunfight with Odell Pickett he'd been happier than he ever imagined he could be, and he'd all but forgotten the trouble with the railroad until Jack mentioned it again. Things at the Circle C had settled into a comfortable routine. The Texas and Pacific was running its rails around the Triangle Bar. The U.S. Marshal looking into the affair had taken Harding Carruthers away in irons. The Christoval sheriff had resigned his job and moved west to parts unknown. Will Dobbs had taken his rangering to another part of the state, so the marshal claimed.

Best of all, there was Sara. Last week he had moved his gear into the house, after a ride over to Knickerbocker for a visit with a preacher. Sara Clay was now Sara Spoon on the official courthouse records that kept track of such things.

Right at first, the idea made him weak around the knees. Then, like a green colt getting used to the feel of a saddle, the notion suited him. He'd made her a promise, to be the best husband he knew how, which wasn't much in the light of his experience with it. But when they rode the Circle C together, and when he held her in his arms, he knew he could make good on his promise. With a woman like Sara, it would be easy.

He stood up beside Sara and took her hand, giving it a little squeeze. For the first time in his memory, things were working out like he wanted them.